A LOW DIVING BIRD

LIBBY COPA

A LOW DIVING BIRD

This novel is a work of fiction. Characters, events, and places, even those that are real, are a coincidence, a product of the author's imagination or are used fictitiously. The author took liberties with historical and regional details for the needs of the story. Historians, please be forgiving.

Thank you to my friends, family, and teachers that supported me and this story throughout its journey.

I gratefully acknowledge YoungArts for their support of *A Low Diving Bird*.

Cover photo by Katie Moum
Cover design by Desert Animal LLC
Formatting by Enchanted Ink Publishing

ISBN 978-1-7351183-5-2

FIRST EDITION

DESERT ANIMAL

For my mother

A LOW DIVING BIRD

LIBBY COPA

"No one has a right to tell you how to live, especially when they come into your house uninvited."

-Jamarquis Alaire Royal

CHAPTER

ONE

MARLOW

Autumn, 1865

We are already ghosts.

They say the war is done. But if the Unionists found us—if we came out, hands up, saying if you forgive, we will you—they would string us to the nearest tree, ring us and then say they are in accordance. That the forgiveness begins now. If my sister Hester knew what we've done, what we do, she would bow her head and offer up the rope we used to swing into Tired Dog River.

What Quantrill taught us is that revenge will distract you from righteous reasoning. What Quantrill taught us is that violence may beget violence, but in stillness you are haunted by your bad doings. I tell myself I do it for the safety of Hester and—though I know it isn't justified—when it comes to those you love, assurance that they will be safe is all that matters. And your damned soul is worth it.

They say the war is over but the fighting is not done, not here. It is easy to say the war is done in the North. But when you live in Missouri—a place that was always divided, its own individual mess—you can't go home to a town, to a place where you got one half of the road quarrelling against the other.

It is night and we are approaching the small plantation. We tie our horses in two groups on different ends of the property. The four of us, Royal, the Lewis brothers, and I make our way through the long grass and assemble on the back porch. The wind simmers and the heat keeps even the crickets' sound smothered. There is a deep northern sleep in this home and we aim to quietly surrender it.

The Lewis brothers go in first and up-quick their boots in unison like a little army attacking the flight of stairs to the main bedchamber where they pull the Reillys from their dreams. Have them kneel beside their beds as if in prayer before they, mirror images of each other in stance, put matching copper bullets into their skulls.

The Reillys' son was one of the first to lead the Jayhawkers in Basque County and Mrs. Reilly went around talking of how proud she was of her son after his death by us rangers. And what we do, our profession now if you will, was to show what you got when you joined with the invaders. Across the prairies, family by family we weigh their loyalty to the old ways. Mr. Reilly freed his workers and had he not, maybe there would have been someone to intercept this attack, would have heard the long click-click drag of our boots on the porch wood. But as it was, there wasn't anyone but us to witness the death of the Reilly family.

The youngest Reilly, the last child left on this plot, Miss Lila Reilly appears at the top of the stairs having heard the boots, the yelling, the pistol shots, and the Lewis brothers ransacking the bedchambers for doubloons. They are like pirates, looking for brooches for their mother and dresses in the latest Paris fashion for their sisters, or perhaps, as it's been rumored, even for themselves.

Lila in her long white nightdress, thin blond hair that falls just to her shoulders, cheek rosy with youth, looks down at me alone, Royal having gone to the kitchen for eats. I'm studying a painted picture of the Reillys when they all were still alive and together under this roof. She makes a murmur, like a question. I sigh. This girl will raise her future children to be against us. I lift my pistol up and shoot her. She falls to the ground as softly as she had come from her room, one arm rests over the top steps. The shot brings the brothers out. Royal from the kitchen.

"Let's go," he says as he slumps a bag over his shoulder. And the brothers come down on call, tame-like, the second of them stepping on the little girl's hand as he passes by her body. The bones surely breaking, no matter.

We cross the field in two groups like a separated pack of lions. We will meet up at our spot and cook a meal by the fire before the smoke can be seen at dawn. By then we'll have vanished.

No matter, we are already ghosts.

CHAPTER

TWO

HESTER

When Hester Cain woke from dozing in the garden between the tomatoes and snap peas, the Yankee soldier was standing over her. The man was in a dark sack coat, with his musket strapped to the soft knapsack that hung over his shoulder. It was his infantryman's uniform trousers, the unmistakable blue color she associated with worry, that made her rise and back away from him.

"You don't need to come any closer," she told the soldier.

The man was still only feet from her. Hester instantly had that feeling in her gut that she should never have traded the gun. At the time she'd done it because they were starving, but now that situation seemed a whole lot better looking than this one. The soldier removed his forage cap. Hester tried to glance out across the field to where it edged up to the woods without the man noticing. She hoped the orphan boys wouldn't take this moment to return from the creek.

"Where are you headed?" she asked him. So rarely did someone just happen by this house, and any persons coming down that road was a cause for worry. People had stopped coming down that road except to make trouble.

"Nowhere in particular," the soldier told her.

"Well, this needn't be one of your stoppin' places on the way."

Hester didn't have a gun, so she wasn't fooling anyone and she knew it.

"Your man at home?" he asked, but when he didn't glance at the windows of the small house, Hester wasn't fooled either.

"You know I don't got no man here." She widened her stance in the dirt between the crop rows. "Do you know who my brother is?"

The soldier told her he did not and rubbed his fingers along the brim of his cap in his hand.

"Just so we're clear on this—my brother Marlow is known in these parts for killing men like you." She wasn't sure if the threat of the Bushwhacker carried much weight anymore.

"Alright then, we're clear on that," the soldier replied. "And since we are hacking at the thicket, I want you to know I am no threat to you."

"Don't be surprised when I am not assured by just your say-so," Hester said.

The man wiped the sweat from his brow. Even though Missouri's autumn sun hadn't rose enough to break the clouds, as if it too was weakened by war and death, and the season had begun to cool, the soldier was perspiring.

"Perhaps you hadn't heard, the war's been done a few months now," he told her.

"I heard."

"So as I said, I am no threat."

He went to take a step toward her but halted when Hester said, "You're a threat because you're a man and you know it."

The soldier lowered his head. He was about the same age as her brother. Perhaps a little older. He was almost a head taller than her and, despite his broad shoulders, he was a lean man. His brown hair was cut short, but the ends curled up slightly. He had a cleft chin. He was handsome, she noticed that too. Hester wanted to know what she looked like to him. She wondered if he saw her as a frayed twenty-year-old girl. If the soldier could tell she wore the same dress every single day of the year. A decade-old pattern no one was wearing in the cities anymore. If he thought her unrefined, as her darling Kip had described her as they were growing up together, because he disapproved of her always allowing her long black hair to hang down around her and because she unapologetically bared her shoulders in the warmest season.

That thought was displaced as Hester caught sight of Steven moving smoothly and with surprising speed for his short legs across the field. The child was between Hester and the soldier in seconds, yelling at the soldier to stay away. Frantic, Steven, the oldest of the orphans who had come to live with her a year ago, bent down and reached for rocks to throw. At first the stones were small and the soldier just put out his hands and laughed as the rocks hit him, as if they were in a game of snowballs.

"Hold on there, boy," the soldier called.

But Steven didn't stop yelling and throwing. Tears streamed down his flushed cheeks.

Hester reached out and touched the child's back. "Stevie, stop," she said, but without force, momentarily struck by the tender feeling of having someone around to play protector. Steven picked up a large stone and before she could reach around his tiny body and clutch him to her to make him stop, he let it go. It hit the Yankee in the face, sending him toppling over. The pack he carried sprawled about him as he fell. Hester put her arms around Steven and held him close to her. The other boys, Aaron and Lonnie, darted across the yard to them to see the commotion. They all stopped and gawked at the fallen soldier. Hester had survived the war on very little, selling most of the belongings her family owned, and the thought ran through her mind that she would now be killed because of the temper of an eleven-year-old boy.

"Oh, Steven," Hester said as she let go of him and moved slowly over to the soldier. He was lying on his side away from them. She bent down and as she was about to touch him, he groaned. She jumped, then quickly knelt beside him and turned him over on his back. The rock had hit him on his left cheekbone. There was a small cut and it was swelling up. He squinted when he looked at her. His eyes were rich blue with specks of brown flint around the iris. He didn't remind her of anyone she had ever known and she found that comforting.

"Come on," Hester discovered herself saying. "We'll go clean that up."

"Don't help him," Steven whispered.

Hester extended her arm to the soldier as he began to stand, in attempt to make amends. They made their way up the steps to the back door of the house. Hester held the door open for the shaken man and she gestured to the boys still standing in the yard.

"Please bring his belongings inside."

The soldier sat down at her small round kitchen table. Hester brought the washbasin over and set a rag in front of the man. He stared at it a minute, as if he did not know what to do with it. After a moment he brought the rag to the water and then to his face. Hester stood against the stove. She felt the adrenaline caused by fear start to slowly leave her. The boys entered the house and set the stranger's pack by the door. They moved to different points in the kitchen, circled around the man, Steven standing between Hester and him. Hester put her arms on Steven's shoulders and pulled his back against her chest. He would be taller than her soon enough. The tears on his cheeks were drying.

"I didn't mean to scare you," the soldier said.

"You didn't scare us," Hester replied. It was an obvious lie, but it made the boys puff out their chests in a way they had never done before, little bodies filled with pride.

The soldier nodded his head and continued to dab his cut with the rag.

"You are not from around here," Hester stated.

"No, I am not."

"Where are you from?"

The soldier offered that before the war he was born and raised in Lawrence.

"I was born in Lawrence," the instantly excitable six-year-old Lonnie burst out, taking a step forward.

"Oh, yeah?" the soldier turned to him. They both looked like they wanted to ask each other questions about their hometown, but neither said anything more about it.

"You are walking in the wrong direction if that's where you're headed," Hester told him.

"I don't have any intentions to go back," the soldier told her.

"Where *are* you going?" Hester asked.

"Somewhere else," the man said flatly.

"Well, you better get on with it then."

The soldier stood up abruptly. Some of the water slid over the side of the bowl when the table rocked against the weight of the man's sudden movement. All three of the orphan boys took a step toward him.

It was Steven who spoke next. He said, "You know why we can't trust you, you're on the other side."

"I wish it could be different," the soldier said.

"So do we. But it ain't," the boy replied.

"I'd like to try and make it so," the soldier said directly to Steven, as if he was asking permission.

"You took too much." Steven spoke for all of them. Each had lost a great deal; what they had known of family, what they had understood a normal life to be like. But then so had the soldier, which was why, Hester figured, he was in a stranger's home instead of his own.

Hester surprised herself when the words, "You may stay for supper," slipped out of her mouth.

She had waited for years for the war to be over, and now that it was, she wanted to show Steven how they could begin to act like it. The soldier was taken aback but he thanked her. Then he took the rag he had used to clean his cut and wiped up the spilt water.

THE SOLDIER'S NAME WAS EBEN Reed. The younger two boys cautiously took Eben with them out to the edge of the field where it met the forest. There the best wild berries grew. They would return, as always, with the berries cupped in their shirts, the juices from the berries leaving stains Hester would be unable to remove from the cotton fabric. Hester could see them from the house and she looked out the window every few minutes to make sure they were still where they said they would be. Steven stayed on the back porch while Hester worked in the kitchen.

When Hester was a little girl, she helped her mother snap pea pods and mash apples. When her mother died, a few women from the town invited her to their homes to show her around a kitchen, teaching her their family recipes. She was a decent cook now—she could make a meal from stems and dry root well enough the starving would say it was worthy. She hid the good herbs behind a loose wallboard where Jayhawkers couldn't find them, she knew the wild ginger made all the difference.

The hunger pain began to set in as the smell of her stew filled the kitchen. She rubbed at her stomach as if it would calm it. Although she had gone much of the war with this familiar ache, her appearance was not that of one who had spent time hungry. Her arms were strong from chopping wood and she had those childbearing hips that Mrs. Jeremy always went on about whenever they met in town.

Hester wondered what Kip would say if he knew she had a Unionist in her home. Kip would see her in town, but he would never come over to speak to her. She would watch him holding his books under his arm entering the schoolhouse where he was the headmaster, and eye the empty sleeve pinned up around his stump where he lost an arm early in the war after a bullet splintered his elbow. Kip hadn't come home right away, he could have been back before most of the men and boys even left. He could have come to be with her so she wouldn't have been so alone one, then two, then three years. But maybe had he returned right away instead of staying in the army, doing whatever with one able arm, he wouldn't have come to be with her anyway, as he wasn't with her now. He would surely disapprove of the Yankee soldier, as would her family. It would be like flint against steel.

Hester noticed Steven standing in the open door watching her. When she looked at him, she felt in some ways she understood him to his center and in other ways she didn't understand him at all. The younger children were easier to navigate.

"It'll be ready quick," she told him. He stayed where he was.

"I didn't mean to cry earlier," he said.

"No one ever means to," Hester told him. "That's why it is important to pay attention when someone *is* crying."

"I did want to hit him, though," said the boy.

Hester nodded. They all wished for big rocks to throw at their will.

"How can you just let him hang about?" Steven asked her.

"Because he doesn't seem to have anywhere to go," Hester explained. She paused a moment. "And I think all of us here know a thing or two about that."

THEY SAT TOGETHER AROUND THE kitchen table. It wasn't quite dusk but Hester had lit the candles. There were not enough dishes so the soldier used his tin cup and field utensils, and as usual Aaron and Lonnie shared tableware.

Hester put the rolls on a cloth and served the stew right from the pot. They ate in the quiet awhile.

Eventually, Eben turned to Lonnie and asked, "Do you remember that birch in front of Big Tree Mercantile? That store with a dozen colors of sugar candy sticks?"

Lonnie's eyes lit up. "Yes!"

"When I was just a little older than you are now, I was a delivery boy for Mr. Ferris. I ran items all over town." The soldier recalled a time he carried a bag of oats and had it over his shoulder and said he could tell it was becoming lighter but explained that he had just thought he was getting stronger. As it turned out there was a hole in the cloth sack and the oats were slowly leaking out, and a trail of oats led from the back door of the store all the way to the Petersons' farm. Lonnie and Aaron giggled.

"You must've felt silly," Lonnie said.

"Boy, did I ever." Eben smiled. "I wonder if the store is still stands, I haven't been there in a long time."

"I think it probably is," Lonnie told him. "But Mr. Ferris ain't. They strung him up to that tree."

Eben lowered his head. "Oh," he said, and then he gave Lonnie a small smile. "Those candies sure were good."

"They were," Lonnie agreed.

"Did you fight in many battles?" Aaron asked him.

Hester could sense that Eben realized for the first time that Aaron had subtle facial deformities. The boy's fox red hair, so thick Hester could hardly get scissors through it, and his freckled skin had been a distraction, but now the soldier was seeing all Aaron's features. She watched him examine the boy. Discover his eyes, which were abnormally horizontal and spaced out from his flat nose, his forehead large and tilted inward, his top lip much thinner than the bottom. But the boy smiled more than the other two children and Hester could tell Eben found relief in that grin.

"I did," Eben told him.

"Which ones?"

"All of them."

Aaron's eyes grew larger.

"Don't be silly," Hester scolded. "You couldn't have been in them all."

The soldier bared the tired face most wore throughout the war, and his cheek was still swollen where it had met the rock.

"Feels that way," he told her and slowly turned his face away. "Tell me." Eben regarded the children. "Are you learned young men? Are you in school?" The boys shook their heads.

"School is most important," he told them. And Hester could sense Aaron and Lonnie believed him instantly without question. The children had not asked to go to school before and she made no offer because she knew Kip would be there and feared he would have treated her as if they had no shared history at all.

STEVEN USUALLY SLEPT ON THE front porch like a sheep dog guarding the house, but on the evening of the soldier's arrival, he stayed inside to keep his presence known to Eben. Hester knew he tried hard to not fall asleep. He lay on his side with his cheek resting on his shoulder, then would drift off and his head would fall onto his forearm and he would jerk himself awake. He placed himself in front of the sofa that Aaron and Lonnie were asleep on, heads at opposite ends. The sofa was the last soft piece of furniture in the house, a wedding gift from her father to her mother over two decades before. Aaron's feet rested upon Lonnie's chest. Lonnie hugged the legs with one arm and his other arm dropped over the side of the cushion not quite reaching the floor. The sofa was torn and dirty from the boys' use of it as a resting place the last few months.

Hester and Eben sat cross-legged in front of the fireplace, the wood floorboards warping and splinting beneath them. She told him about her plans for a bigger garden next season and he explained how to plant certain vegetables next to each other to create natural shade. It had been a long time since she held a lengthy conversation with anyone other than the boys. The soldier told Hester that tomorrow he could survey the property and then draw her a diagram for creating a more prosperous crop.

"If you'd like me to stay, that is. I could be of use here."

Hester thought about Kip and his one arm—and how he would not speak to her now. She thought of her father and brother who did not return when the war was over. They went on fighting or went on being dead. She thought of her orphans who had picked her. She didn't know if she, alone, could teach them all the things they'd need to know about how to be good. She thought on this soldier and believed that he might know how. He was an idealist. She wasn't raised in a home with that luxury and she was curious about what shift that might cause in the boys, given the opportunity.

"You may stay."

"It really is something that you managed through this war all on your own," Eben said.

"Maybe I didn't manage at all. Maybe I'm dead—we've all died and we are haunting you for any leftover sins you may not have made amends with. Maybe we're all together in the middle world, where those who are not ready to be judged fit for heaven or hell go, and we've got to make it like this before we go on one way instead of the other," she said.

"Perhaps that is the case. I'd believe it could be so," he said.

Eben unrolled the bedding that was strapped to his pack and placed it next to the fireplace. Hester made her way up the stairs to her own room where she slept on the floor atop a collection of old quilts. She took off her day-dress and set it by the bench under the windowsill and pulled her nightshirt over her head. She lay down alone.

She was still afraid of the dark after all this time. When the old house groaned in the wind, she flinched. She tried

to steady her breath by telling herself it was her Pa or Marlow going out to the shed or getting an early start on the
milking. That all these years had just been a dream. If she
couldn't make herself believe that, she would tell herself her
family had come home just now and didn't want to wake
her. She tried not to remember that they had sold the cow
before the war. Hester tried to forget that gentlemen do not
creep around a house. She lay in the darkness and tried to
find light.

CHAPTER

THREE

EBEN

It was a good piece of land, Eben thought, as he labored. It had been largely uncultivated for a long time, but it was quiet and shapeable. The day after his arrival, Hester hardly spoke to him. He did what she needed done simply by walking around the yard and finding work.

He noticed Hester crook her neck from time to time outside the kitchen window, watching him mend the walk-in chicken coop. Lonnie and Aaron went beyond the field into the woods to play by the creek, but Steven stayed behind. He always seemed to keep himself between him and Hester. Hester and Steven swept up then mopped the back porch as Eben fixed the coop roof.

Later in the afternoon, when he was surveying the garden, she came and stood a few feet away from him, Steven at her side. Neither said anything, so he decided to talk to her.

"There isn't time to plant more tomatoes, but we might have another herb crop just yet. Do you have any pots?" he asked.

Hester brought him over to the shed that had been built near the broken corral, a dozen yards from the house. The door hadn't been open in some time.

"What's in there?" Eben asked.

Hester said nothing. She stepped back as Eben pulled the door against its rusted hinges. Steven stretched his neck to try and look past him and see inside. Eben peered in and from what he could see there wasn't much in the shed—a few tools, bridles for stock animals, and old fine building wood that he thought he could put to use.

"You coming?" he asked and stepped in. "Will you help me carry a few of these things to the house?" When he came back to the door holding out the items he expected her to take, Eben found that Hester was making her way back to the house, Steven following behind her, and Eben was left alone again.

Eben had drifted through many towns like the one near Hester's home after he was discharged from the army. Everywhere he went people were hesitant to make the natural connections to strangers that used to just be good manners. It was as if all the survivors of the war, for there are many kinds of survivors, lived life peeling away the feeling of a need to bond, mentally preparing themselves to keep surviving. He was welcome nowhere, forever the reminder of the horror everyone had experienced.

Yesterday, when he made it around the curve in the road, he could see that this house was the end of the route, but he was curious because it looked unkempt and possibly abandoned. It wasn't until he was right close that he saw the garden and then the woman inside it, and he felt the pull.

Now, as the sun hovered on the horizon, he found Hester on her porch chair. Steven gathered twigs in the yard for kindling. As the distance grew between Steven and Hester, the boy remained watchful of Eben's every move. On the edge of the porch, Eben set the supplies he would use the next day to plant a last chance crop. Eben sat down beside the materials and rinsed his hands in a bucket of water. He could feel how winter was inching its way into the land. The leaves had taken a turn. Geese frequently flew overhead. A breath could be seen on the air in the early morning. He picked at the dirt under his nails. Eben felt Hester's eyes turn from watching for the boys to return from the creek, onto him.

"Hester, how long have you been caring for those boys?" he asked. She could not be old enough to be their mother. Breaking her silence, she told him this story.

"First came Aaron; he followed me home one day from town when he saw me in the store trading several articles of clothing for flour. He walked a little behind me the whole way home and stood at the gate when I went inside," she said. "From the window I could see him there knocking a stick against the shabby wood boards of the fence by the road or throwing stones at the birds in the trees. When the bread had risen it was near dark outside. I opened the front door and held it for him, and he raced in toward the smell. He fell asleep on the couch and slept there each night since. A week later Aaron brought Lonnie home. Steven entered our life two months following. He had been caught stealing salt beef at the store and I stepped in and offered to pay for the jerky in his pockets when Mr. Glouson was about to whip him good."

She watched Steven's awkward movements with the kindling. "He guards me now, as I guarded him," she said, with a distant glance. Eben thought, these were her new young men, to replace the grown ones who didn't return.

Eben wondered how long she was alone before they came.

"A handful of seasons," she told him.

He thought it was such a long time, but he didn't say it. Everyone was alone during the war. Even a soldier, who may not be alone in presence, but Eben learned the act of killing is as solitary as they come. It takes only one to shoot a bullet from a rifle. It only takes one to die. There was always talk about unity in war, but every man's death is his own and he never died in comfort, and he never died where he'd rather. Everyone was alone during war and even now in its aftermath.

THE TWO BOYS BROUGHT HOME a small bass that Hester cooked and served with lettuce.

"You have to be careful when you go off into the woods," Eben told the boys at the table.

"We know that," Aaron protested on their behalf.

"You have to be careful of the witches of the deep wood." Eben had all their attention. "The witches live throughout the woods all over the countryside in cabins that blend right into the trees. If you are not paying attention, you can pass right by them without noticing. The trick is to watch for the smoke from their chimneys," Eben warned. "I once knew some little boys who were out in the woods. One called the other a name—one that wasn't very kind—and almost immediately a witch appeared. Gave the boy a chance to apologize, but he wouldn't. So, she cut out the tongue of the boy who said the mean words, the ears of the boy who heard them, and then both their hearts. She cooked them all in a stew." Eben tailed off. "You must always apologize if you say something cruel to someone else, and you have to mean it, for the witch will know the truth."

Eben glanced around the table. Aaron's mouth hung open, Steven leaned a little closer to Hester, and Lonnie looked ready to break into tears. There was a moment of silence.

"Doesn't Hester ever tell you stories?" Eben asked them, surprised by their mesmerized fear. He hadn't meant to scare the boys, but now he didn't know how to take it back. The little boys shook their heads.

"Never?"

"Just sometimes she reads to us about the land," Aaron told him. "About plants and animals and what's beyond the sky."

"Hester, how come you don't tell them stories or make-believe?"

"We have a hard enough time finding truth around here, we don't need to be making new things up."

AS EBEN ROLLED OUT HIS mat that evening, he thought about his mother and the house he grew up in, a home he might be able to reflect into this house. His mother had not been in support or opposed to him volunteering for the infantry. She had not put much stock in the war, believing it would pass swiftly, as once was the common thought of many. Eben's mother had been widowed years and had not used loneliness as a way to keep him, as another might. She was not insecure with the thought of being left alone in her home just off the center of town in Lawrence. She had her projects to keep her busy. She was known as a woman who would take in injured animals or horses no longer able to be used for work or ride. Hester reminded him of her in that way. Eben had wanted to fight to liberate the nation of oppression and his mother said he could make up his own mind. She believed in kindness and forgiveness, which people can sometimes mistake for mixed loyalty.

AT DAWN, EBEN HEATED BREAD for the boys on the stove, and noticed how good it felt to care for them. Acts like this made him think again of his mother.

Hester came down the stairs and found them all sitting at the kitchen table.

"Well, what's going on here?" she asked, and put her hands on the sides of the kitchen doorframe.

"Eben's taking us to school!" Aaron told her.

"Oh, really?" Hester looked to Eben. "Are you so settled in that you didn't feel you should consult me on this first?"

"Do you object to them receiving an education?" He had always been taught that a formal education was the foundation of lifelong prosperity, and although he had been wandering, unsure of his new path after the war, he still felt this to be true.

"No, but—"

"Can we go, can we please?" Lonnie asked, and batted his eyes at her.

For a moment Eben realized he may have misstepped, rushed his influence, but he was thankful when Hester responded to the boy, "I suppose that would be alright."

Steven rose from his seat and came up to Hester. He stood very close to her as if to tell her something privately. Eben had yet to understand how the boy was bonded to her. He was only slightly older than the other two children, but Steven was very aware of the consequences of the war.

"I would really like to go to school," Steven said.

"Of course, you go," Hester said, gesturing for him to be gone with the wave of her hand.

"I would like it very much if you came with us," Steven said, looking back over at Eben.

"I'll be fine," Hester assured him. "And if at any moment I am not, you'll feel it, won't you?" She put her hand to his heart. "And you are the fastest runner I know." Steven nodded, and that was all it took for it to be agreed between them.

EBEN ESCORTED THE BOYS THE mile to the schoolhouse, which sat at the backend of town where three roads converged.

"Will you come inside with us?" Lonnie asked Eben.

"No, you go on ahead," Eben coxed. "I will be here to fetch you at the end of the day."

Eben had not wanted his presence to influence how the students or their headmaster would perceive the boys. He stood in the center of the directional split as the boys ran up to the school with the other children. The town, he thought, was one spark and a gust of wind away from burning to the ground. It couldn't have been made up of more than a hundred people. The few families living down the various roads, as Hester did, venturing in for supplies and news from time to time. The merchant store, the icehouse, the butcher barn, the blacksmith quarters, the fabric store, and the men's tavern that made up the limited offerings, showed no signs of a town undergoing the post-war growth other regions were experiencing.

Eben could feel the residents in the town watching him, judging him by the color of his jacket. In the predominately secesh town he stood out like a black eye. Behind their watchful glances, there housed anger, sadness, or pain. He didn't want those gapes, but he had nothing else to wear. No one would trade for them in the towns he passed through, and Hester had sold almost all of her family's belongings to provide for herself and the boys. There were no clothes left from the men from her past. When the children had gone inside, Eben turned and walked back to Hester.

He had assisted in the occupancy of Nevada, Missouri for many months at the end of the war. He was there with the belief they would be involved in the rehabilitation of the town's government and education programs. But the soldiers were just there to enforce the law, hunt guerrillas, and court the single women and widows. Eben wanted to start somewhere fresh when discharged, not return to Lawrence where he would know all the people who had stood by and watched as soldiers tainted Union law and forgot God's laws. But he hadn't come to a town where he had not seen the same thing as he had in Nevada. Towns were being occupied, not moved progressively to reform. Eben saw how he could help Hester's house rebuild itself, and he found consolation in that.

When Eben returned to the house, he found Hester pickling cucumbers. On their first full day together the young woman hardly said a word. However, the day that followed was the opposite. It was as if she tested what it was like to be in discussion with someone and then after going without it again, determined she'd much rather have the former, even with a stranger, even under the circumstances.

"Hester, is there any money?" Eben asked.

"Does it appear to you that I am holding on to anything I can spare?" she said.

"There's none?" He put his weight on one hip. "The boys are going to need paper and more books," he told her.

"For what?"

"Learning."

Hester looked over her shoulder at Eben. "You could trade the stool there but then we'd have to squeeze tight at mealtime. I suppose you could take the inside doors off and sell them and the hinges."

Eben surveyed the kitchen door. He noted the metal.

"Will you write your mother that you have stopped here when you have paper?" Hester wondered.

"I suppose not. Momma was killed in Lawrence."

Hester nodded. "My momma is dead too. She died when I was little."

"Of illness?"

"You could say," Hester told him. "She hung herself out in that shed."

WHILE THE BOYS SAT TOGETHER in the school pews, Eben saw to the crops. He went to work on creating a transportable garden that could be brought in and out of the house when the hard frosts began. Hester came and offered him a cup of tea in the early afternoon. The gesture was not lost on him.

"Remember what it was like before the war?" Eben asked Hester.

"Not really," Hester told him. "War's been going on out here a long time. Maybe they were quieter about it in the city, just talk. But out here, people have been fighting amongst each other long before the States called for it to be so."

"There must be things that you remember from before," Eben said.

"Of course. But the memories are not the same anymore," Hester told him. "They're spoiled."

EBEN WENT AND COLLECTED THE boys toward the end of the day. They were playing together in front of the school. He asked if they enjoyed themselves and they said that they had an awful lot to learn. The war changed the possibility of education for everyone. There was the new embracement that schoolhouses should be open to all. He suspected Hester's boys would not feel too far behind the other children, as many were new to academics. He did have some concern for Aaron. The boy had unique intellectual characteristics he had not witnessed before in a child. Perhaps they might hinder his growth.

On the walk home Lonnie fell a little behind the others with Eben. Lonnie told him that their teacher had one arm and another of the schoolchildren said that Mr. Evans had lost the other in the war fighting the North, and that most Confederates weren't allowed to be schoolteachers any longer.

"In that place of all places, it shouldn't matter whose side you were on," Eben told him.

"What about at home?" Lonnie asked.

A tight smile formed on Eben's face. If Eben could put a smell to sadness he would say that it smelt like a field of burning cotton.

"You don't worry about all that," he told the boy.

After another moment of walking, Eben felt that there was someone following behind them. The road wound itself through the forest, and it wasn't until they were on the last stretch of the road near the house that the man behind them came into view. Eben urged the boys inside and asked them to send out Hester. He grabbed the rake and started going about gathering the fallen leaves in the yard. When the respectably dressed middle-aged man approached the house, having shown himself to move at an unthreatening stroll, Hester was standing on the porch holding her bowl of mashed squash.

"Mr. Jeremy," Hester greeted the man when he came through the gate. "Is there any new word on my family?"

"No news," he told her. "Hester, what's that man doing here?" Mr. Jeremy asked as he gestured at Eben.

"Raking is what it looks like to me," Hester said. She had such sturdy words for someone scared of anyone coming to her door.

Mr. Jeremy and Hester locked eyes. Eben understood the man's gawk conveyed the silent words like "Trouble" and "the Cause" and "Yankee" and "indecency". And in Hester's blank stare she appeared only to ask him to go away. Mr. Jeremy, a gentleman still in these times, turned and strolled back to town.

When he was out of earshot Eben turned to Hester.

"Is there something we should talk about?"

"I don't know, is there?" she asked. She beat away at her squash some more with the wooden ladle. Eben set the rake against the house and came up the first porch step.

"There's talk," he said.

"There's always talk," she supposed.

Eben took the last steps and stood facing Hester.

"Hester, you must not ever be ashamed," he told her. "You are an extremely capable woman." He reached out and removed the bowl from her hands, and gently touched her skin as he coaxed the ladle from her grip.

"Who are you?" she asked, but it wasn't the kind of question that needed answering.

CHAPTER

FOUR

AARON

He did not wander and tried to remember all his chores.

He liked blackberries best, how they puckered his lips.

He wouldn't stick his fingers in the sugar and salt and lick them.

He wouldn't touch the bread until it was cooled.

He would help fish at the creek.

He would help carry the firewood.

He wasn't to stick his hands under bushes. Snakes.

He was to share the couch with Lonnie. Make room.

He was not to leave the house without saying where he was going.

He was to come right back to the house if he heard

strange voices or horses or saw someone that didn't live in the house.

He did not think of his before family. He didn't want to think of his before family because this was his family now.

There was so much to remember.

CHAPTER

FIVE

HESTER

ester would rise in the night, light a candle, and go down a few steps of the stairs and check on the boys. She often worried those first few months after they arrived that they would suddenly up and leave in the night or that she had imagined them. But since Eben arrived, she felt secure that they would all be there when she rose with the dawn. She beheld each one in turn and listened to their soft breaths.

They were all sad stories. Aaron's parents had traded him away to pay a debt on their land, but the boy skipped out like a bird off to find his way back to the home he lost direction to. Lonnie spent every single year of his life with war. He knew North and he knew South, though he was not old enough to have witnessed the great divide. He had no concept of oneness. He had been passed around. People dying on him was like a tradition. And Steven, who was mute on his past, was shaken to the core. Eben came to them now as a strange uncalculated gift.

After picturing what the boys' lives were like before the war—before they found their way here—Hester returned to her room and thought of Kip before falling back asleep. She didn't understand why she was not enough. She never fancied anyone else.

Kip was more educated than nearly anyone in town. He was less wild than the other young men. He preferred a good book to a big social gathering. He had always been serious, so very serious. She tried to get him to be playful, but he never caught on. She told herself that did not matter to her. He was a learned man and always had intelligent things to say. He made her feel smart when he shared his knowledge with her. Other girls chased the boys around the schoolyard, grabbing them and kissing them on the cheek. Hester always stood on the edge of the grounds, acting the part of the future wife of the future headmaster, for she was certain she would marry Kip Evans someday. She was assured she would need no other prospects, no other dreams for the rest of her life.

Now, faced with the fact he might never even speak to her again, she wasn't sure what to do with herself. It seemed impossible to make up a new dream, for she had lived so long with the idea of him. She didn't want a ring on her finger to flash around to the girls in town or at the tea parties, not that there had been one of those in some time, they pulled

away from her during the war as the Union gained promi-
nence in the town. She was invited nowhere and no letters
arrived. She wasn't looking for a husband to drive the horse
and new carriage to church on Sunday and have people say
they were so prosperous, she was so well kept. What she was
looking for, what she needed most of all, was a man in her
home and bed and heart—and that was all. That is what she
wanted for herself most. Someone to speak the last line at
night and to greet her at dawn. Someone to ask her about
how her day had been and recall a shared memory.

Kip never paid her sweet compliments. He never said,
'Hester, you are a pretty girl. Hester, your eyes are intense
and beautiful.' Which she was, and they were. She knew she
had a uniqueness to her, and she had—when you pulled it
out of her—a quick attitude and a smart tongue. She wasn't
funny in a comical way but there was always a cleverness to
her. And she was sure Kip saw all of it, but he never brought
himself to say it. Instead, his compliments had been; 'Hester, you are good at spelling but you should know your
mathematics better. Hester, you write thoughts fine, but
you need to work on your penmanship. Hester, you sewed a
good dress, but green is more your color.'

Growing up, the thing that assured her that they would
one day wed was that he never appeared to have eyes for
anyone else. And he would tell her that too. "Don't you
think for a moment I am seeking other prospects," he'd say.
She'd translate it as best she could into something romantic
in her head. They also made plans together of the life they

35

would one day lead, and that was what she clung to now. Plans were like promises, and they had made a lot together, and it was hard to let go of a dozen promises all at once. He'd been gone long stretches before, when he went off to private school before the war, but this was different, because even though he came back to town he was still gone.

Sometimes she thought of Kip touching her between her legs with his hand, that lost hand that would never touch anyone again like that because it was in the ground or out in a field somewhere or in a bird's belly. She would fall asleep with her head and heart like a bees' hive, full of both honey and stingers.

Hester was in the pumpkin patch trying to find the ripest pumpkin because they needed more to eat. In the weeks since Eben's arrival, they were able to double their rations. But the chickens were quieting their laying season and animals were still getting into the garden, even though Eben set traps—something she had never learned to do. Occasionally, on a good day, a rabbit would find its way into one. But not today.

The pumpkins had not grown large but there was a small one ready for eating, though it would hardly feed them all. Hester thought about how the vegetable would have fed her well when she was alone. How she'd have dried the seeds, roasted them up with spice, eaten them for days, but with the others in the house each portion would be less. She had a moment where she wished she was alone but then she took the thought back. She threw imaginary salt over her shoulder and then wrenched free the orange ball.

She stood with the vegetable hanging from its stem in her hand and she looked off in the distance where the road bent around the cove of trees and on toward town. That first winter alone she had gone three months without seeing a person and without going into town to make any trades. The whole world could have dropped away and she would have no idea, it was almost as if it had. She ate watered-down stew or oats for every meal. Hester was surprised she hadn't gone crazy. She slept twice as much as usual. She shut herself down so she wouldn't go into fits from missing her family so badly. She would spend long periods of time trying to call her brother Marlow home in her head. She would tell him she missed the dependable companionship she had with him in her youth. Sometimes Hester believed he could hear her and was just being stubborn to spite her, and she would get furious at Marlow for it. Studying the empty road before her, she tried to call him home, but after all this time she didn't wait for a response.

Hester held a constant hope that the Jayhawkers wouldn't bring the dead to her as they sometimes did. Cow heads on the front porch, horse intestines strung along the fence, and that one time a man, hung upside down in the tree across the road, throat cut, blood slowly dripping out of him. When she left the house to see his face, days later, she had known him. He was a local Confederate ranger. He had come to visit her from time to time, to make sure she was still breathing. Now he was up in her tree. She couldn't pull him down by herself. She had to leave him there watching the birds go at him as he began to rot. Eventually his skin fell away from the bone and he slid through the rope he was tied. She dragged his body as far from the house as she could, which wasn't too far, and buried him near the bones of the horse she killed before the second winter.

HESTER FIRST NOTICED STEVEN TALKING to himself before Eben arrived. Once in a while, when she'd be watching the boys in the field, Steven would separate from them and she would see him talking away. He was still young, she told herself. She knew people talked to themselves—her Pa often repeated his daily tasks aloud to himself, and Marlow would sing or hum as he did his work. But she hadn't figured out what he was really doing until Eben told her. What she hadn't realized was, while out in the field or that night she heard him say to himself on the porch, "Shhh, go to sleep, it will be better in the morning," he had been talking to a ghost. It was when Eben mentioned it that she identified Steven's words were in conversations with a shadow.

"That boy thinks he's talking to someone," Eben said, putting the dead frogs on the kitchen table across from where she was working through the pumpkin guts.

"He does that sometimes," Hester informed him.

"You know what I'm talking about then?"

"Steven."

"Normally, I'd think, so what? Thing is, Hester, that boy hears someone talking back."

Hester called Steven into the room. He hovered in the doorway like he did. Eben sat at the table and used his Sheffield knife to remove the skin from the meat.

"Stevie, have you got someone with you?" Hester asked, flat out.

"No," Steven said.

"Because it appears to me like you are talking to someone. You sure you don't have anyone with you?"

"No," Steven said again, then added, "not right now."

Hester wanted Eben to say something, but he didn't have words either. Steven asked if he was in trouble and Hester told him of course not.

"My brother said if you cut the pumpkin slice in fourths first it will make easier mash," he said, and then he walked back outside, door swinging.

After a moment Eben spoke. "My grandmother used to say my grandfather was still around after he died. She wouldn't let anyone call her a widow." Eben explained that his grandmother never remarried and that she talked to her dead husband all the time as if he were there. "She talked right to the air. She would say things like, Albert, hasn't he gotten tall? You like the sugar cakes too, don't you, Albert? I think the thought of him being around was almost like having him there. Maybe that's what Steven is doing. Or maybe his brother is there. Maybe these things happen."

Hester clenched her jaw. She balled up one of her hands into a fist at her side. "Maybe your grandmother could have been happier if she fully accepted he was gone and then she could have been with someone else."

Eben thought and then said, "Maybe the idea of him was good enough."

A WEEK LATER WHEN EBEN left in the morning to escort Lonnie and Aaron to school, Hester opened all the windows in the house. She knew it was the last days before a real cold would set in. She was cleaning the fire pit in the living room when she saw Steven's figure appear in the open window nearest her. He leaned half his body inside the house, resting his stomach on the sill and letting his arms—which were growing faster than any other part of his body—dangle down and touch the floorboards.

"Do you want to talk about why you didn't go to school today?" Hester asked.

"I just didn't want to," the boy told her.

She swept at the soot with her brush. Working it out of the cracks between the bricks. After a few minutes of him watching her, he nonchalantly said, "My brother thinks you have a nice face."

Hester felt the goosebumps crawl from the back of her neck down her arms and her fingers began to tingle.

"Did your brother have a lot of girls chasing after him before the war?" she asked.

"He did."

Hester couldn't bring herself to look at Steven. "And he thinks I have a nice face?"

Steven corrected himself, "He said you have a kind face."

"Not a pretty face?"

"He always says kindness is beautiful."

She found herself sucking a breath in between her teeth.

"He says that it's alright if you go around barefoot, you are too good for anyone to judge you for it."

Hester brushed the fallen cinder into the black pail and carried it through the kitchen and out the backdoor. Steven came around the side of the house and caught up with her to walk across the field to the tree line to dispose of the ash.

"Steven," she found herself saying. "You know, I have a brother and I talk to him sometimes too."

"You do?"

"Yes. He comes to me in my dreams," she confessed. "Sometimes I ask him about things I don't know about and he tells me if he knows. Sometimes if I don't know how to do something and I ask him how, he tells me to teach my-self—which is what he used to say to me all the time when we were growing up."

They came to the woods and Hester dumped the bucket and they turned around to return to the house. Hester didn't remember much of her mother, but she remembered her saying that no matter what happened in this land, Marlow would take care of her.

"I know that it is hard to imagine what it would be like to never see your brother again. There are even whole moments you forget that he isn't here," she said.

Hester reached down and took the boy's hand in hers, for her own comfort as well as for Steven's.

Then under his breath she heard him say, "But my brother *is* here."

They heard the horses before they saw the riders. The Jayhawkers were intrepid in their announcement as they came down the road. Hollering to one another and giving off war cries. They were at the front gate before Hester and Steven could reach the back porch steps.

"What should I do?" Steven said. Hester wasn't sure it was her he was asking.

"Don't be too bold," Hester spoke soft but firm. "Don't give them any reason to take anything from us."

The first of the men were already letting themselves inside the house when Hester and Steven made it to the living room. Through the open windows she could clearly see that the men tied their horses where they pleased around the yard, breaking the gate off its top hinge even though there were whole sections of the fence missing, used as firewood in the winter, that they could have walked their horses through. They were dressed in long coats that they buttoned up to the neck, guns holstered around their waists. Their short-brimmed hats held a feather to the left side. A few of the men removed their hats when they entered and saw Hester standing there. Their hair was cut short, a feature that distinctly separated them from the Bushwhackers who she knew to let their hair grow out long. Hester counted seven. There wasn't much for them to knock about, and their search of the house ended quickly and the Jayhawkers gathered in the living room. Hester would not release Steven's hand, they stood side by side. Between their hands a prayer for a Copperhead among the men.

One of the men asked Hester where the other boys were and she told him. Another asked her if she had any milk and she told him they did not.

A man came down the stairs from the second floor and asked, "Where is your brother?"

She recognized him. In school whenever they had been arranged alphabetically Hester would be placed beside Cody Brinson. He could hardly bring himself to glance at her back then, turning flush in the face when having to ask anything of her, now he moved around her home freely ready to demand without pause.

Cody came closer to Hester. "Where is Marlow?"

"She doesn't know where he is," Steven said with loud, unyielding volume. Hester was able to pull Steven behind her faster than Cody was able to reach him. As Cody came closer to them, they moved backward until Steven reached the wall beside the fireplace and Hester couldn't push him back any further.

Cody's face was close to hers. He smelt rich of sweat and horse. He asked again, "Where is Marlow?"

Eben walked into the house then. He had been so quiet about his entry that everyone just turned to face him when he spoke.

"Can I help you men?" he asked.

After a brief pause, the Jayhawkers drew their guns and had them pointed at Eben. Hester could tell he was not fazed by the men, though she thought he should be. He remained so calm. He set down his satchel next to the door and moved to the center of the room. He let them get a good look at him. Perhaps it was his Union trousers that gave him away or maybe it was just his confidence, standing like a man who knew his side had won.

A Jayhawker asked, "You're a soldier?"

"I was."

"What were you fighting for?"

Eben rubbed his hands together slowly. "A way of life I thought was right."

There was the sound of a hammer clicking back.

"North or South?"

"I fought for Kansas. For the ideals of President Lincoln," Eben told them. "I fought with the Kansas Volunteer Infantry."

The Jayhawkers began to lower their guns, a few stood in an embarrassed manner as if they were about to be scolded, and would not make eye contact. Hester felt relief try to take over, but she wouldn't let it.

"We didn't know she was your lady. We were mistaken about this plot, we were told there would be graybacks here," one said. "Our words aren't for you."

The men started to exit the house offering their foolish regards.

Cody turned back to Hester. He was so close to her their energy sparked off each other.

"I still know who your family is, Hester. I have an elephant's memory," he hissed. "I won't forget anytime soon, no matter what strays you take in."

He backed away from her slowly and strolled from the house. He was the last to mount his horse, and unlike the other Jayhawkers who trotted their horses away from their land, Cody Brinson walked his mare down the road.

Hester took a step forward. And then another but she found Steven's hand and hers were still locked and he was staying where he was.

"You need to let go of my hand now, I have chores to do," Hester said to the boy and broke from him.

Hester walked through the kitchen. She heard Eben console Steven, and Steven tell Eben to leave him alone. She went out the back door and Steven the front.

Hester stopped by the shed. She collected the empty pail she dropped when she heard the horses, but set it back down on the ground as she stood before the abandoned shack, trying to figure out why everything happened the way it did, what it would have been like if just one moment in her life had been different. What would have been the outcome had Eben not arrived home when he had?

Eben came from the house and stood behind her.

"Your mother's not still hanging in there," he said.

"In my heart she is," she told him, not turning around. "I want you to take it down. Take it apart. Sell what you can."

"We need to talk about what just happened. Don't avoid it. It could have been a lot worse."

She turned her head and glared at him over her shoulder.

"It has been," she told him. "This wasn't the first time." Her face softened. "I have nothing. Nothing I can't give up. Nothing that wouldn't fill me more than the price I could get for selling it."

"You got those boys there," Eben reminded her.

"You know what I really mean."

"I do."

Hester started to cry then and not wanting him to see her weakness, she turned her face away from him. She heard Eben take a few steps toward her and then she felt his hands rest on her sides just above her hips. She caught her breath but when she let it out it caused her tears to fall with more urgency. Eben leaned forward, arched down, and placed his forehead against the back of her neck. She could feel the warmth of his breath pass through the thickness of her hair and land on her skin. Hester allowed herself to stay in that moment until she collected her composure, and her own breath came out smooth and steady. She reached up, wiped her cheeks, and turned her body so that Eben was forced to move away. One hand remained touching her. She hooked her loose hair behind her ears.

"I admit," Hester told him. "I liked being called your lady."

"Is that what you are going to take from this day?" he asked, amused.

Hester moved completely away from Eben.

"What do you suggest?"

"I am so pleased you felt that way, but we should also discuss the threat they offer."

Hester picked up the ash pail and then pointed to the shed. "Knock it down."

THAT NIGHT, AFTER DINNER, EBEN pulled out a deck of cards and invited all the boys onto the porch to learn a game.

"Are you going to teach our boys to be gamblers then?" Hester asked him.

"It's good to know a trick or two," Eben told her.

Hester carried the collection of their potted plants into the house and then sat down on the steps and looked up at the sky lit with little stars. She thought about Kip being so close in distance, that if she lit a big enough fire he would be able to see it. Hester had begun to feel like nothing she did would bring him down that road.

"Eben, what did you see when you saw me for the first time?" Hester asked the soldier. "What was your very first thought?"

He shuffled and dealt out the cards before he spoke.

"Thought your hair resembled a river of raven feathers."

AS THE HOUSEHOLD READIED ITSELF for slumber, Steven lingered on the porch with no intention of coming back inside until breakfast. Hester left an extra blanket for him by the door and then she waited until she was sure the boys were asleep before she stoked the fire one last time and started up to her room. Eben watched her from his mat across from the sleeping boys, his back against the wall. Hester stopped after a few steps and Eben glanced up at her. All she did was cock her head in the direction of the top of the stairs, and he rose, and came to her on the steps. He followed behind her almost touching the base of her back with his hand, but not quite.

MARLOW

Winter, 1866

Dark and cold we have become all the way through—the backs of our necks with that constant feel of someone's lips blowing on us. Collars up high, shoulders hunched. If we stayed in any moment long enough, we'd turn to stone and they'd find us one day and call us relics of a lost cause.

We made winter camp at the Clarences', a small plantation out by nowhere, and go hunting when snow is absent so we don't leave tracks back our way. We stay in the hut where their slaves had been housed and sometimes I think I hear singing on the wind when the moon rises full and reflects onto the ground, a low mournful sorrow song of a forgotten something. Mr. Clarence had gone and shot his slaves. Better they dead than free working for some man in the North, was how he said it.

My companions, the Lewis brothers, sometimes go off two or three days at a time, where they go, I can't say. Royal thinks they go into the wood because they are more comfortable as a duet than as a posse. Sometimes I think maybe they ride all the way to their family home in Benedict Township to have a meal with their mother and then turn right around and come back. Maybe just needing a kind word, remember what they're doing this for. If I could get to Hester that fast and safe, I'd be satisfied with just a glimpse of her.

Last time I saw my sister she was throwing a tantrum. She was no young girl yet there she was stomping her feet down by the creek as I set off, yelling that if I don't come home that instant she was going to reveal every secret she ever kept for me, and she does got a hold on me.

I became a scout for many months after. I've died many times. I walked right up in places—long dark hair tucked up hoping I don't have to tip my hat to say ma'am. Hester see me with my long locks, she'd tell me I am too pretty now. In Lawrence we killed some, and I watched as they executed Pa. Reminded me of a dog catching a bird in flight, swallowing it whole. How do I tell Hester that?

On this night, like most, I sit on the dirt floor near the fire and look over a few of father's things—his cup with his initials engraved, his work gloves, and his pistol. As I aged people told me I looked like Pa. After several months away from home, those we met couldn't peg us as related. I had grown a heavy beard, whereas he stayed smooth-cheeked, I became thicker with strength in my whole body, and he went the opposite. This war hollowed him. My regret is he will not see Hester again, that he left this earth feeling he did not do enough.

"You're thinking fathers are supposed to save their children," Royal says, coming and sitting over. The large brim of his riders' cap shadowed over most of his face. "Fathers are supposed to shield."

Jamarquis Alaire Royal was a French drifter who somehow found his way to this bloody land war. His words sound like they want to linger there when leaving his throat and hitting the air. I run my thumb over my dead Pa's initials engraved on the tin cup.

"Fathers are supposed to give a future," I say. "What future do I have when my skill has become killing? Who teaches their child such a thing?" I have never said these thoughts aloud before. Royal has a way that makes you feel he can already see your insides.

"You see, we did something bad in a past life," Royal says. "We were put back here in the South to make it right and yet we never made it right, so we are paying for it, for this life's wrong and all the wrong from the times before."

I ask Royal if he can see the future as well as he can read the present and know our past doings, and he says he just makes guesses on the assumption we all continue to act as we've always done. But if I wanted to know some future, he knows a girl who's got eyes for that sort of thing.

Keegan Lewis holds the reins of his brother Decker's horse and guides it along with us. Decker hadn't been keen on the idea of venturing out into the night to find this seer of Royal's, but this kid has the uncanny ability to sleep just about anywhere, so he crawls up on his mare and shut his eyes as if there's nothing to it.

I can see the muscular veins that protrude from the strong hinds of the dark brown almost-filly I got off a sorry Bushwhacker not long ago. I liked the star pattern on the front of his head like a brand. He is a quiet horse, which is good for the job we have. I keep him a foot or two away from his comrades at all times. If he stands too close to another horse, he has been known to nip.

Keegan observes that this forest we make our way through would make good hiding as spring was closing in, but Royal puts a finger on his lips and says hush on such things. "These woods play for keeps."

The sun's low rising but we can see there isn't much to be had when we arrive at our destination. This woman's cabin is broken down. Walls slowly peeling away from one another, wood splintering, waving with watered age. There is a fire burning inside. The door opens and she is the kind of woman to dream about—but she is a shape-shifter looking old in light and young in shadow. Her hair like a chameleon, changing with her movements between red, golden, and silver.

"Aimee," Royal says, and dismounts from his horse.

"Jamarquis?" her sweetly husky voice calls back. Like Royal, she isn't from this land.

Royal steps forward and they look each other over. She comes a few paces from her door. He removes his hat, his long hair flowing down around his shoulders. She takes a strand of it between her fingers with one hand, stands on her tiptoes, reaches up and cups the back of his neck with the other. The most intimate moment I have ever experienced, yet it is not even mine to hold. After a spot, she steps back from him and regards us inside.

The soup she gives is watered down, so as to feed us all, but it's warm on its way to the belly. Decker isn't shy and asks Aimee where she got her powers. She sees it not as power, and I tell her I believe foresight to be the most powerful of things. Says she, "I was given my ability the way you were given the color of your hair upon birth. Perhaps it has always been that shade, or it has changed, strengthened or faded."

Royal goes to work fixing things outside her cabin. The brothers are first and I step outside with Royal. I can hear them laughing and making a ruckus with her.

"How'd you find this place?" I ask Royal and watch him bring hammer to wood on the side of her cabin. I put my hands under the armpits of my coat for extra warmth.

"I knew her before," he says, and I assume he means the war. Royal and I have followed in the same direction for going on over three years now, but I know little of his history.

That's not to say I don't know the kind of man he is. He just isn't one to talk on himself as a piece, only as part of a whole, a bigger collective of spirits. Royal and I go to our individual silences. I think on Hester. I tell her about where I am. I describe the sycamores and their colorless limbs that are reaching down with the weight of winter toward the earth. I describe the sun, which is at its most golden at dawn slivering through the thick wood. I tell her I believe that Royal means something more than kindness when he mends this sibyl's house. I would like to know the story behind it all, I say to her, but I am unable to request the unnecessary. I tell Hester all these things even though she isn't around, and I hope her heart hears.

"You sending up a prayer to that songbird of yours?" Royal says without turning to face me.

"I willed her a thought," I say.

When the brothers come out in good spirits, I go in for my turn. Aimee pours me a cup of tea as I sit. The room feels smaller with just the two of us in it. "They are content as pups," I say. "You must have told them good news."

"I did," she said. "But I was lying. Then I did other things so they wouldn't ask no more of it."

"You going to tell me lies too?" I say, leaning back in the chair.

"If you want me to entertain you in other ways, I can do that instead." Under her skirt she turns her knee outward, making her dress look like a fan.

"I want to know the truth," I say.

"Are you sure?" She is gazing into her teacup and I wonder what she sees in it.

"Is there no good left?" I ask.

"Tell me why you are here. What is it you want?"

"I want to protect a girl," I confess.

"Your love?"

"Yes. My sister," I say. "She is love."

"She's not alone," Aimee tells me.

"She's not?"

She makes a motion with both hands, that of wiping something off the table that sits one inch in the air.

"You're here, aren't you? All the things in the world and you are here asking on her."

"Is that enough?" I ask.

"It's only the first part of it."

Aimee goes to her washbasin and begins to scrub her hands.

"Those are the words you have for me?"

"For now," she says. She offers a faint smile. "It isn't time for the second part yet."

We stay at the cabin until the sun is down again. Royal and Aimee whisper their goodbyes to one another.

"We shall see each other again soon," she says to me and I don't doubt it.

We make our way through the brush heading east. Just as we break onto the road we come upon them—a group of Red Legs talking with some Jayhawkers resting their horses. The four of us stop and look at the group of them and they look on the group of us. Who draws first it's hard to say because their bullets seem to reach us just as ours reach them. There are more of them to be sure and so we let out of there in an instant, but I have two pistols at my hips ready to fire, and one on my boot and my rifle strapped to the rump of my steed, that I aim to fire back as we make our way gone.

We light out and reenter the woods, the dense brush with narrow developed paths, the beech and service berry grow thick in patches, the sudden slope of ground held by sphagnum moss breaking under hoofs, for that was our ground and it isn't a common one, this is our territory, and we know how to let it shade us in a way those outsiders do not. They are in larger numbers, and they sound like a thundercloud behind us tearing down the forest in their chase.

I know the sound when a man is hit. I can even tell the difference between a good hit or bad, and I call it depending on if I am doing the giving or the taking. I can tell the sound of the bullet into Keegan's flesh is one of the ending kind. Decker is hit also but not too bad. The moon doesn't appear through the trees. What I see is like a blind man. I go on a learned instinct. My horse is my guide. I feel the shot like a bee sting graze across my shoulder blade. Not a bullet that deserves too much thought. Royal grabs on to poor Keegan's reins and urges that horse to stay with us. We dig deeper into the brush and the thunder falls farther and farther behind.

We circle back to the Clarences'. The stars sprout in the sky above the plot. We bring Keegan inside and lay him down on the floor. Decker goes and lays beside his lost brother, draping one arm over his still chest. The long exhales of my breath stretch out before me in the small room. Royal checks on us wounded and tells me mine is nothing but a scratch, that I'd had worse and that's to be sure. Then he goes and sits out in front of the shelter to keep a lookout. I am left with the brothers. As I rest my eyes I hear Decker's soft mourning cry for his brother as if he too was lost, and it stays always in the background.

When I wake Royal is carrying Keegan's body, wrapped in a bed sheet he must have been offered from the main house, past me. Decker is already on his horse. Royal lays the dead boy across his mount, as Decker holds the reins for his brother. They are situated for leaving. I go out to them.

"I'll bring them to their people," Royal tells me. "Then I will see about meeting up with the others. I shall send word." He throws rope to crisscross the body's back and ties it under the horse's belly.

"I'll get my things," I say, and turn to the hut.

"No," Royal says. I think I heard wrong so I keep going but then stop after a few feet.

"What's that mean?" I ask. Royal stays silent. "What am I supposed to do?"

"What did Aimee tell you?" Royal wonders, mounting his own steed.

"She was vague," I tell him.

"Then you weren't listening right," Royal says. "Go home."

SEVEN

EBEN

Eben lay on his side curved next to Hester on the pile of quilts on the floor. The presence of winter lingered longer than he had ever known it to. The long winter left the land gutted and bruised as they all were. He and Hester took turns at night going downstairs to coax the fire that kept the boys warm. Most nights, although indoors, he noticed his breath on the air when he exhaled.

The initial fear of intruders lessened when there was fresh snow, but as it melted they would go back to listening for sounds that were trying to hide themselves. The Jayhawkers made the occasional appearance in town to show they kept a watchful eye. They helped themselves. They were strong as a group, individually they were just like everyone else. Steven had begun to act out in different ways since the incident with Cody Brinson and the intruders; he would refuse to do a chore, go off by himself into the woods, or return from school midday with no explanation as to why. Eben tried to act as Hester did toward him, in a way that showed not indifference, but patience. Eben wondered if girls were taught this manner of softness, the way his father and then his uncles taught him to be a man of honor, or if it was just their nature. He couldn't say he'd ever met a woman who didn't show signs of it. But he'd known all dispositions of men. He wanted Steven to trust him. To understand, even if Steven would not fully have faith in him, that Eben only wished to help the boy through whatever it was he was struggling with.

What concerned Eben most presently was that his things were being moved. One day he couldn't find his suspenders, but then a few days later he found them hanging on a doorknob where Hester said she had not put them. The next—his knife was found in the salt bin. When he dug it out at breakfast the boys all laughed, but none would give up the prankster. It went on like this. Sometimes it took him awhile to find what was missing. He would search all over and then find it right on the table in plain sight. It was the cap that was the most mysterious. He found it one day atop a snowbank in the field with there being not one footprint but his own leading to it. He had little to take but he felt someone else's fingers all over his belongings. After all his personal items were hid, what would be taken next?

"Someday, someone could come for the boys," Eben said to Hester, as he lay beside her.

He felt her shift against him.

"Who? Who will come?"

"I don't know. A relation. Then what will you do?"

"What could I do?" she asked. "Things are the way they are. There's a reason they're here. There's a reason you're here too."

Eben watched the side of Hester's body next to him rise with each light breath she took. He reached out and rested his hand on her hip. He knew they kept some of their histories from one another and that there were thoughts that went unsaid, and he knew they were both fine with that for now. He quickstepped with a few girls in his youth. He'd doe-eyed and weathered them and for that he was only partially sorry. What he thought of was how playful he had been. There was innocence in that dance and he missed that part of himself that had been hopeful, that had been one for romance. He had, in those years in war, felt that he was drowning and it was not until he saw Hester, those boys, this house, that he felt a luster inside of him of that man he had hoped someday to become. But still, things were kept unsaid for the sake of moving forward, some things were kept just for one's self.

Eben had not told Hester of the occurrence that had taken place when he brought the boys to town to pick out their holiday treat, that he had walked up to pay for the boys' candy and the storekeeper said, "Your coin's no good here." And at first he had mistaken the man as offering a gift or implying he would add the sweets to Hester's tab for later when the times were sorted out, but when the boys stopped opening their first candies, he knew it meant the sugars weren't for them, that they were unwanted and unwelcome, takers without offerings.

"You want me to have the boys put them back?" Eben asked.

"I do," the storekeeper said.

"You tell them then."

"Put the sweets back and get out," the man yelled at the children.

Eben leaned in and reminded him, "These are Hester's boys."

"Right now they're with you, and you ain't welcome."

Eben moved away from the counter and went to the exit and opened the door. The boys put their candy in his hand as they passed him to go outside—so close to getting a small gift just to have it taken back. Eben held the door open for Mr. Evans, the boys' schoolteacher, who entered simultaneously as the boys departed. He eyed their little cast-down faces.

Eben returned to the counter and put the candies on the wood top. He also put a copper-nickel on the wood and then another coin and another.

"I am buying that candy," he insisted.

"No, you ain't," the shopkeeper said.

"No, you are not," Mr. Evans corrected the man. "No, you are not," he said again. He made his way up to the men. "Use proper English if you say you run a proper establishment."

Slender in form, the teacher was not an intimidating man, but his words were strong. Mr. Evans slid one of the coins closer to the clerk. "Run it like a gentleman," he had said. "Don't punish the children for the actions of the man." The shopkeeper grabbed the coin and Eben took the rest back and put them in his pocket with the candies. He nodded obligingly to the educator and left the store. He didn't need to trouble Hester with small events like that.

There were things Eben might have to keep from Hester always, for he did not want to be that man no longer, or simply because he did not have the right words to utter about such things. He had killed in battle, he made widows of women and although the dead soldiers might forgive him, for they could relate to their shared experience of taking a life, he knew that their wives could never. They lived in loss, where the fallen men were just gone. Hester did not need to be burdened by this, or the fact that he sometimes heard the whistle of a cannon and moved from where he anticipated a shell was to land. He couldn't tell Hester that he was sometimes embarrassed to be on the victorious side, for there were those in town who still treated him as someone who was now claiming a prize for all he'd done, and that he had started to lose confidence in the Union victory when he first entered her house.

But then, through the hardship, there were good times. Like the one day where Eben wrapped Hester in her brown wool shawl, covered her eyes and guided her outside into the yard. The boys giggled and whispered last-minute details to each other. Lonnie took hold of two of Hester's fingers and led her to the perfect place for her to stand. When Eben removed his hands, Hester stood in front of a snowwoman with rock eyes and lips, with twigs for arms, at which the end held her mittens, and around the waist was tied Hester's apron.

"Merry Christmas," they offered.

EBEN ROSE AND WENT DOWNSTAIRS and added another log to the fire. He happened upon this house and this girl and her orphans by chance. He could have gone one way or another but he found himself in that yard on that day and she was there and that was all it took. At times he thought life better than it could have been had there never been a war. Made him believe in something again, if it was only this, a home filled with breath.

When Eben returned upstairs, he stopped at the window to look out. His breath steamed up the windowpane when he leaned too close. A light frost collected around the frame. In the yard Eben could see the ghost of a man near the remains of the snowwoman. Eben could tell by the way the ghost lifted his legs high that he was a soldier; it was the walk that echoed having traveled great distances in march. The ghost was carrying logs between a woodpile and the fire pit, but the brushwood would vanish when he laid it down so his fire could never catch and he could not get warm.

CHAPTER

EIGHT

MARLOW

I descend on the house after the sun is down. I have been watching since dusk showed the first absent colors of darkness. Several figures passed by the windows but I couldn't make anyone out for certain 'til I saw a woman. She came onto the back porch to dump water from a bucket and it caught the cold air and steamed before her. She stopped and looked out at the woods for a moment, right where I stood, as if she could sense me there, and then went inside.

Now in full dark, I walk my horse across the field and tie it to a tree. My steps make sound and leave wet marks where I move on the back porch. Laughter and muffled voices seep through the walls and I unlatch the door and go right inside.

I startle the group having dinner. The man pulls his chair out fast and stands to confront me, 'cept he has no weapon but the spoon in his hand. Three young boys sit clumped together around the table and then there is Hester. My Hester. We take simultaneous deep intakes of breath then catch them. When we can't hold our air any longer, we say each other's names. After another pause all I can think of to say is, "My boots are wet," to which she tells me to take them off and she'll put them by the fire.

Hester gets up and I can see her whole frame. She moves smoothly and softly. Hester appears much like a mix of our father in his later years and what I recalled our mother to look like. In my thoughts of her these warrin' years I never pictured this woman before me, I never suspected a few years was all it took to change a person so. But who would understand better than I about such things?

I set down my pack and I clumsily pull off each boot, feeling all the eyes watching me as if their eyeballs are pressing into my skin. I hadn't been gone so long that these boys belonged to my sister, I assure myself. Hester takes the boots from me and leaves the room with them. In my damp, holed stockings I stand in the awkwardness of it all. The man steps forward, offering his chair to me. I notice the color of his trousers and he notices me noticing. One beat I have my pistol on him.

"Marlow." Hester's voice is a solid soldier of meaning. She is in the room again holding my boots to her sides. I turn away from the man for just a moment and I catch Hester's eye. "Don't do that," she says. I holster.

"If I am not mistaken, you are a Unionist," I say. "Am I correct?"

The man gives a long nod of his head. Hester gestures for him to take her place at the table, and as he does, she departs once more. I go sit in his chair and look across at the little boys' eyes on me. They are cautiously curious. Hester returns and reaches in the oven and pulls out two hot rolls as if she had expected me. She leans over and puts them on the plate before me. She brings her arms around my shoulders and down my chest and hugs me in this position. She is grasping on strongly, but her body feels rigid, as if she doesn't know me. All I can do is reach up and touch her forearms. She slips her arms loose from my hands and steps away from me. She goes to sit with the man, sharing the chair with him.

"I am glad you could join us," Hester says.

"I am glad to be here." It sounds like a small thing but it isn't.

The kitchen room is much the same but the cupboard is empty, where both Mother's and Father's sets of family china had been when I left. In the corner of the ceiling where the walls meet, it looks as though moss is growing. It is simply mold from water damage, but it appears as if the earth is taking the house back, slowly, as if no one has been living here for years.

The most grown of the boys, rude with intent, watches me too closely.

"What are you staring at?" I say.

"Who are you?" he asks.

"This is my house. I live here."

"This is *our* house," he responds. "*We* live here."

"This is my brother," Hester tells the child, softly. "He built that chair you sit on when he was your age."

"Who are you?" I return. None of the boys respond. No one speaks. As if no one knew the answer. There is a hollowness in this silence, and it is lasting.

AFTER DINNER WE MOVE INTO the front room of the house. The man Hester calls Eben goes out to secure my horse for the night. The room is bare bones. Hester offers me a seat on the sofa next to two of the boys. Where has this house gone? The wood has not been polished in a long time. This was my chore once. I would polish the stairs and the banister early in the morning without telling Hester, who would then be forced to stay on the second floor as if it were a tower, unable to come down until the wax set.

"Marlow," Hester asks, cutting in on my moment of full memory. "What was the ocean like? Was the water cool or warm?" I realize I have not brought her any treasures from my time away and now can't even indulge her curiosity.

"I can't say. I didn't make it farther than Tennessee," I tell her.

"All this time, you didn't go but feet away?" Hester appears stupefied. "Why I can whistle as far."

I want to tell her that I heard her, but I say nothing.

"Why have you not come sooner?"

"It was not safe," I say.

"It was not safe with you absent," my sister replies.

"It was impossible," I try to tell her.

"Nothing is such," says she.

The man reenters and he stands next to Hester. He removes his leather work gloves and presses them together. He goes to the fireplace and rests the gloves above the mantel. He smoothes them flat. Eben speaks in a low voice, the pacing of his words spaced out. "Tell me, Marlow," he questions, "have you ever been to Lawrence?"

"I have," I say, knowing what is passing between us.

"Recently? Since the war began?"

We are lock-eyed. We are inching closer to each other without even moving.

I ask the Yankee, "Shall we have words?"

The man looks briefly at Hester, then a delicate divergence seems to settle in with the man. My hand is ready with intent and all he says is, "No. There aren't any."

"You sure you don't want to go ahead and get this out of the way?" I challenge. I want him to fight me before I know too much. My instinct is to be happy for my sister, and my instinct is to kill this man.

Hester takes me up to the room that had been ours as children. Where I read to her aloud all the histories in the storybooks. It is bare, as if nothing had ever been there. Hester disappears across the hall to our parents' room to join the man. I unclasp my mat that I hadn't expected to still sleep on once I returned home and roll it out where my bed had once been. I hear Hester's soft footsteps return to the doorway. She stands there a pause before she speaks. My girl that's now a woman. I wonder how she sees me, if she can still see me as I once was.

"Marlow," she asks, "is Pa coming home?"

"No, Hester." I tell her the truth because there is no use making up a story now. "He is not."

"Oh." She turns and leaves the room once more.

I lay down and put my hands behind my head. About to let myself sleep when I hear it. I know that sound from my youth, but it is thick and deep now—the sound of Hester's cry. I bolt right up from the floor and tear across the hall without even reaching for my guns—my bare hands will be enough to channel the strength of a Goliath. Bursting through the door I find Hester sobbing on their quilts on the floor. Eben is beside her with his arms wrapped around her, trying to calm her. When Hester sees me in the room she starts in with a new batch of heaping sobs. I kneel beside her and wrap my arms around her as well. We are locked in an awkward embrace, the three of us. Air thick with the smell of smoke, cedar, chicory, and grief, of course grief.

After Hester falls asleep, I slip my arms out from around her and leave her with Eben, who rubs her back in tired circles. I head to my room and collect my satchel then go down the stairs. I had missed so much of my life. I come back to a man in my home and my sister caring for three children. I watch the boys resting in the front room, and my thought is this—one is old enough to fight, give another year the middle one will be ready too, and if I start now, what a killer the small one could be.

THE ROAD THROUGH TOWN IS empty for it's deep night but I stay on the side paths. I go to the headmaster's cabin. I try the backdoor knob but it won't turn. I go around the front of the house cautiously. The knob also doesn't give. I hear a quiet, shaken voice come from the other side of the door.

"Who's there?"

"It's Marlow," I say, hushed.

The door cracks and a sliver of Kip's face appears. He looks a minute at me, then the door opens wide and I slip in quickly. I notice Kip has his rifle propped up beside him. He looks out in both directions and then, satisfied, shuts the door, and slips the locks in place.

"Does anyone know you're back?" Kip asks.

"Yes."

"Do they know you are here?"

"No."

I look over my friend that I haven't seen in a handful of years. Kip is in his nightclothes. He is worn and missing something, but still presents himself the part of the head-master we all watched him groom himself to become. He still holds the presence of a man who deserves a good woman's love.

"Why aren't you married to my sister? Why instead is there a Yankee and a flock of orphans in my house?" I question outright.

Kip jerks his head as if suddenly startled with insult. "That's why you're here?"

I invite myself over and lean against his eating table.

"I am making talk," I say. "You rather I ask you how you get to go on livin' in this cabin and go down the road in the open after being such a patriot of the Cause that you were?"

"I go with my own small group of fears," he tells, and tries to pretend he is relaxing some by crossing his one arm over his chest, resting it on the alternate hip and leaning against a small writing desk near the door. We hold for a moment. We used to have so much to say when we saw one another every day.

"You hear anything?" I finally ask.

"The war's over, Marlow," Kip says to me.

"Is there anyone in this town I should see to?"

Kip shakes his head.

"It's over, Marlow."

"Is it?" He is making me feel unwelcome so as I move to leave out the back, I say, "Seems you're missing something." I could mean the arm that is no more, or the fire that he doesn't understand is still spreading.

Kip sees me out the rear door.

"It was good to see you, Marlow," he says. And stalls there with more yet to say. He sighs deep, as if he doesn't want to say what spills out next. "Mort Henry recently returned having served as a sergeant under a Union general."

I DO NOT HAVE TO go far to reach the Henry plot. I tie my horse right to a porch post. There is a flat staleness to the air. A musk smell. The cottage is small like Kip's. Not too much to look at. I kick the door in, am in the bedchamber shooting fire before Mort Henry has time to reach under his bed and cock his gun. His blood splatters across the blanket and part of the wall. I go back to the other room and take the food from his pantry. I fill my pockets with this and that. I fill a canvas sack with goods. I could take more. I could take it all. But this will do.

NINE

HESTER

Hester watched through the kitchen window as Marlow walked across the back field to the well. He lowered the bucket by rope down deep and brought it back up full of cold mucky water. She watched him dump the contents of the bucket over his head. He didn't make any cry when the icy water met his skin. He shook his head and the water fell from the long strands of his hair. Marlow brushed away the pieces that stuck to his face and locked them back behind his ears.

Hester was unable to read him as easily as she could before. They had been capable of talking to one another without words said aloud. Sensing the other's reaction before it was given. She believed they were connected as people spoke of twins having a link between them, conversing in their own language. The war had taken everything.

That morning Hester had come into her kitchen and discovered the table full of provisions that appeared overnight. The little boys devoured a portion of the food before Eben took them to school and the remainder of the items still lay exposed in front of her now. She'd forgotten what this kind of abundance was like. Hester had not touched anything for fear it was cursed.

There was a time she was so desperately hungry she wouldn't have been able to question any food's arrival. She thought of how, this time last year, the boys' faces twisted at the taste filling their mouths—the rusted water flavor washing down the spoiled vegetables. She added pinches of rosemary to the catfish but it had not suffered to disguise that unmistakable flavor of death. Hester allowed herself to feel sorry for them all. Sorry she had them eat such a meal, sorry they could do no better, sorry they were all not with their real families, eating, safe. Hester had done something then she had not done since the winter she shot the horse—caused an impulsive death. She rose and went out to the chicken coop. She opened the coop door, grabbed the nearest hen, brought that bird into the yard, twisted its head free from its body, and then she took it inside. The boys, still seated, watched as she plucked the feathers, gutted the bird, quartered the meat. They sat together quietly at the table while it roasted. In the tired darkness of night, three young boys and a young woman ate the entire hen, filling their bellies in ways they could not remember knowing.

Now she looked at this partial feast wondering what to believe and what to long for and what would be the repercussions for wishing for more than enough.

Marlow came inside and sat down in a chair across from where she stood.

Hester felt the same sensation in her gut come over her that she had at times around Steven. A gnawing feeling in her insides she couldn't shake. Hester recalled how Marlow sat outside the door of Kip's room at his uncle's boarding house. She and Kip could be left alone together there, but she was always aware of Marlow perched nearby in case she needed him. She could see the shadow of his swinging legs move back and forth in the space between the door and floor, as he sat on the balcony railing waiting for her. It was the same feeling she got then. That feeling that he was on guard.

"Hester, you sit down and you eat," Marlow commanded, and Hester found she followed the order without question, as she would have done blindly in her life before the war. Hester bit into a raw potato. The sound of an uncooked potato was just like that of an apple and Hester pretended what she ate was that.

"You know Charlie Baxter was killed?" Hester told her brother.

"I know."

"And Samuel and Troy?"

"Yep."

"Miss Fisher had her house burned by Jayhawkers and with her whole kin gone she went to be with her cousin in Texas."

"Texas is the place for the going."

"Marlow, are you home for good? You were gone a long time."

He smiled at her, with no assurances, and she returned it.

"Tell me Hester, what you hear of Kip?"

Hester didn't miss a beat when she responded.

"Can't say."

"Oh no?" Marlow leaned back in his chair. "So it wasn't him, that one-armed schoolteacher I saw in town?"

Hester shrugged, as if they were talking about any old acquaintance.

"Maybe it was him," Hester said. "You want to talk about what you've been doing these past few years?"

"Not particularly, no."

"You know I almost starved," Hester told her brother.

"I was shot sixteen times," he rebutted.

"Is that true?"

"No," he admitted.

Hester thought that the tension would release from her chest when Marlow returned, but it was just as tight as it had been on the day he left. She feared this was how it always would be. That the ease would never come. She worried she would not be able to suffer it indefinitely. Hester thought of her mother for just a moment. She knew it was only a question of who would come first. Which army would stand on their steps and whom would she invite inside when she was given a choice.

"Why didn't you just go to him?" Marlow asked her. She knew whom he meant but still she played dumb.

"To who?"

"You know very well to who," he said, calling her bluff.

"A good man could devastate you, but he won't," Hester said. "Did you do all those things they said you did?"

"Yes. And some. But what they have left out is they done them too."

HESTER HAD PUT ALL THE stolen goods away in the places they would have gone had they been theirs and was watching vegetables stew. She had spent enough time alone to gain the patience to simply wait for something to happen—like watching the plants in the garden grow or like this, staring at the supper slowly come to fruition in a pot. Marlow was in the field beginning to make a corral for his horse from wood left over from the demolishment of the shed. Eben came and stood beside her.

"You know a man by name of Mr. Henry?" Eben asked.

"Sure, Mort."

"He was killed last night."

"Thieves?"

"That's not what they're whispering."

"What are they sayin'?"

"You know what," Eben said. "And Hester, if I am hearing it, and people don't talk to me, you know who else will hear it mighty quick if they haven't already."

HESTER WENT BACK INTO TOWN with Eben later in the day to retrieve the boys. She wasn't certain she should leave Marlow but she also wanted to keep on with the routine in case anyone was paying attention. She collected eggs and put them in a basket to trade. When they were out of view from the house Eben took the basket of eggs and carried them for her. He took her hand.

Most of the townspeople kept their distance from Hester during the war, for everyone knew who her father and brother were, and though their sons in fact may have been with them or died in their same fight, her name was the one they knew like Quantrill or Anderson. They wanted no part in it if it meant they didn't have safe passage. Before the war people in the town sought her father for advice. They were welcoming even when her mother went and took herself from the earth. She never heard anyone say a word about her Pa that wasn't kind. Hester was proud to be the daughter of such a man. The folk in town did not know what to make of her stance beside the Yankee soldier. There was a recovery from the war going on and for many that meant pretending like nothing happened, like nothing was happening. Hester and Eben could come and go together without any real altercation. Although, she suspected the talk of her now was not always fine.

Eben went to the schoolhouse while Hester brought her eggs into the butcher's barn. She set the basket on the exchange table and Mr. Jeremy flipped back the holding cloth. This was not an item usually exchanged, but Mr. Jeremy always made exceptions for her family when he could.

"There isn't much for trade," Hester told him.

"And we know the reason."

Mr. Jeremy started to take each egg out and checked them over.

"They're all good," she assured him.

"Still have to check," he said.

He pulled each egg out one at a time and, satisfied, laid them on a cloth, displaying them like they were precious gems.

"I heard a thing this very morning," Mr. Jeremy told Hester hesitantly. His body was rigid, and his eyes flittered down when they met hers.

"Speak your words."

"I was told by a credible source that your brother may have returned."

"Now wouldn't that be something?" Hester said.

"It would be, indeed. I wonder too if Cody Brinson shouldn't start looking over his shoulder."

"I'd like to know a person who hasn't been looking over their shoulder for the past several years."

"What a way for a lady to speak," Mr. Jeremy said, and he shook his head.

"There's no lady here."

"Could have fooled me, Ms. Cain," he said. "Do you want smoked goat?"

"That'll do."

"If there is any message to get out, I still have ways to put words on the wind."

Hester understood he was expressing his loyalty to the Cause and she appreciated his risk. She thought the language of war was a habit, spoken more gravely after time.

Mr. Jeremy went down into his cellar and came up with an arm size of meat that Hester knew was worth more than her hen's eggs.

"My Pa is dead," Hester found herself saying.

"I know," was Mr. Jeremy's response. "I didn't have the words to tell you."

"You could have just said my Pa was dead."

"And then what?"

WHEN HESTER EXITED THE SHOP, Eben and the boys were waiting for her. Lonnie had crawled up and was being carried piggyback by Eben.

"Steven had to sit in the corner at school today," Lonnie tattled.

"Why so?" Hester asked.

"He talked back to Mr. Evans," Aaron told her.

"Steven, did you think you were in the right?"

Steven nodded.

"Alright then."

Hester started their walk for home.

"He shouldn't have gone against his schoolmaster," Eben expressed.

"I am sure he had good reason."

Hester followed her thoughts into a memory of when she was younger; Marlow, Kip and her would play in the schoolhouse after all the other children were gone. Kip would pretend to teach and Marlow and Hester would take turns being the good student and the bad student. When Hester was very bad Kip would slap the palms of her hands with a ruler and make her sit in the corner with her back to them. When she was good she was rewarded.

THEY ALL SQUEEZED TOGETHER AROUND the kitchen table for supper. Their meal was plentiful and filling. Hester's heart beat like a war drum for those she loved. It was almost like living a normal life, she thought, 'til Steven turned to Marlow.

"My brother says you have to be careful being so close to town," Steven said. "There are creepers all about. You included."

Marlow surveyed the other children. Hester felt herself ready to react, to protect the boy.

"Which one is your brother?" Marlow asked, regarding the children.

"Neither."

"You're troubled."

"My brother says the same of you."

Hester could see Marlow's hand flinch slightly, as if he was about to smack the boy.

"Marlow," Hester said, catching his attention. She shook her head and he seemed to lose his thoughts.

HESTER STOOD BESIDE HER BROTHER as they cleaned up from the meal. She washed the cookware and dishes and Marlow dried them with a cloth and stacked them together on the shelf. They did not speak. There was a familiarity to this task done together like no other. Although she had missed her father and Kip so very much, she knew it was Marlow she missed the most.

Kip once said to Hester that he saw her as a Mrs. Evans and sometimes referred to her as such when they were alone. She had grown attached to the title and when he said it her heart hop-scotched. There had been no official proposal but her father told her that he had given Kip his blessing for them to marry whenever they were ready.

She knew that she had not gone to confront Kip, to address whether she was ever to become a Mrs. Evans again, because a part of her was certain that Marlow would come home, and he would handle things with Kip. He would make it right.

"I thought you'd do more," Hester heard herself say aloud.

Marlow read into her thoughts, and knew her meaning. "Just say the word."

EBEN AND HESTER WERE SITTING at the kitchen table early the next morning, drinking tea before the sun started to crawl into the sky. They were speaking in low whispers about nothing in particular when Marlow came in the back door with his duffle bag over his shoulder like a Kris Kringle, a hunchback, a heavy loaded beaver. He began unloading the goods onto the table. Hester and Eben watched him for a moment in silence. Hester told her brother he had blood on his shirt.

"Don't look at that. It's nothing," he said.

"It's not nothing." She stood up and got a rag from the wash bin and walked toward her brother. "Did you cut yourself?" Hester knew even a small cut could fester.

Marlow brushed her away from him with his hand.

"Here, let me look at it," Hester tried.

"It's not his blood," Eben said, not raising his eyes from his cup.

"What?"

"It's not his blood, Hester," Eben said again.

Faster than words could leave a mouth, Marlow had his gun drawn and the barrel pressed against the center temple of Eben's skull. Hester gasped.

"And what of it, Yank?"

"Are we back here again?" Eben said softly.

"Marlow, don't." Hester put her hand on her brother's shoulder, but he felt no weight from it.

"I thought I might just shoot you," Marlow said to Eben.

CHAPTER

TEN

MARLOW

I turned my horse down through the gully and over to the Walters' plantation. Crawled through some dead harvest and watched the light move across the windows. All I could make out was the widow Walter and Black Benjamin, who everyone knew wouldn't ever leave her—even after her sons went off to fight and their Pa died, Benjamin didn't run. I saw the dark man in the house, but I didn't see the sons. I don't kill loyal slaves. I went back into the woods, through the hills and down a deep ravine to a meeting shack that was for Bushwhackers once upon a time.

A light was on inside. I approached cautiously on foot. Two horses were tied to the hitch post and two soldiers were seated at the table playing cards. But their hair's short. Union army-issued coats draped over the chairs. They were taking refuge in what is ours. My first shot hit the man facing the window. The bullet deflected off the window glass and hit the man lower in the stomach than I planned. The second man whose back was to me only had time to gauge what happened to his companion before I planted one in his back. The first man fondled his wound and the horrific realization that he might be about to die when I entered the hut. The place was empty 'cept for the men and their sacks.

"You got anything worth having?" I asked the soldier, who was loudly mourning the lot of blood spilling out of his belly, praying to some god that wasn't going to do nothing. "Quit your carrying on."

Each man's sack held several pounds of tin rations, more than would ever be issued to individuals. I started to search through the pockets of the man bleeding out and found a picture card next to his breast. The man reached for it, but I smacked his hand away. He was defeated easy, and went back to holding his insides inside him, while I examined the image.

"This your wife?" I asked. "She's only a little pretty."

I dropped her on the ground. The man reached helplessly down for it. He doubled over, his fingers just about to grasp the woman's likeness, when I slid the card further away from him with my boot.

"Should have thought a little harder about what could happen to you if you came here to try and tell us how to be," I say. "Now your woman's going to be missing you."

I relieved the dead man of his gun, shot the breathing man in the head, then took his pistol. I grabbed their sacks and left the place.

I untied the horses and slapped their rears, "Be free," I shouted, but they didn't trot away. My good horse and I headed at a slow trot toward home. A short distance from the ravine I heard hooves stomping behind. I stopped to hide in a collection of clustered maples. After a minute a horse passed by, without a rider. It stopped when it could not make my trail. In the dark I saw the second horse stopped behind the first. The horses of the fallen soldiers had trailed me from the shack. They were trained to follow. That is what they knew. I went back to my trail and carried on. I let the horses follow. Hester would find them grazing in the field.

I COME FROM THIS PATH, yet find myself unsatisfied. I want to shoot the Yankee sitting at my table having tea with my sister.

"If you think on it just a little longer, I reckon you'll change your mind," Eben says of my known plan to kill him.

"Why's that?"

"Because I don't suspect Hester will like you killing me too well," Eben says, calm-like, even though I have a gun pointed square center of his head.

"She'll get over it."

"How long do you think that'll take, Marlow? How do you think she will look at you afterward?"

"I don't like your manner of talk," I tell him.

"You'll get over it," he responds and stands up and goes toward the back door. I find I can't shoot him in this particular moment.

THIS IS HOW PA DIED. After Lawrence there are two sides to the guerrilla's coin. Those that wanted to fight like a land army and those that wanted to fight like a sea army. In a land war there are rules of engagement. There is the boundary of respectful discord. At sea, anything goes, there is only open water with nowhere to fall. For both sides of the conflict, there were two sides within them each. And the conflict was more unpredictable for those that brought the ocean to the middle lands.

Small groups broke away in the night to go fight in their own gang, or join the army, and our father was ready to do similar, make for the coastal battles, but I wanted to wait it out and stay with the pack. We were arguing about going this way and that when we were overheard by a commanding leader, who in less than a blink, had Pa on his knees and shot him in the head for planned desertion. Next was me, but as I moved forward to attack him rather than sit down and take it, Royal came up behind the man that shot Pa, and put a bullet in him the same. Maybe my comrades knew that if they crossed Royal, he would have his witch put a hex on them. In these times, as in all war, you don't want to go into battle with a hex on you. It's hard enough to go into a fight with your own Jonah than to go into war with a witch's spell on your plate as well. You will end up eating all kinds of dirt, and likely the worms and maggots will be eating you soon enough. So that ended discussion on the matter and I set sail with a new posse of rangers so to speak.

EBEN ASSISTS ME IN BUILDING a horse corral. We keep the children between us and say what we need through them. This labor is hard on my body, where before the war it was what my muscles knew well. The mud that coats the ground is the same as I've known it, and there is no other like it. We slide around in the slick wet clay.

Hester sits on the back porch and I watch the boy Aaron go and take a place on the step below her. My sister begins to run her fingers through his hair. Her fingers work between strands of the matted red locks like a comb. After some time of this, the boy tilts his head far back and smiles at Hester. She pats his head lightly, a gesture a mother would make to her child. Although I don't feel my bond with Hester has lessened all that much, I cannot remember what the simple connection, passed through a touch, can radiate. My hands always turn violent.

CHAPTER

ELEVEN

STEVEN

Are you there?...I did as you asked. Why are we doing this?...He seems nice enough...Hest...Hester says...but Hester says...Hester says we'll be okay. We are safer now that he is here. And Marlow is here now too. We aren't as hungry...Eben is lying to me?...If it is a trick, it is a mean trick. Why does he do it?...What does he want me to believe?...How do you know it is not honorable and true? How will I know?...What if you're not around to tell me?...How will we take it all back?"

CHAPTER

TWELVE

HESTER

As Hester walked through her garden, made up of just the first hint of sprouts, she thought of the dream she had during the night. She dreamt her arm had been severed from her, as Kip's was in battle, and that she found the boys using the limb to hit a ball around in the field. The dream had spooked her, but then she settled into the rationale that she and the children could find use for just about anything these days.

Hester knelt on her hands and knees to inspect the buds that were beginning to grow, and then decided to lie down on her back on the cold ground. She did these things, acts she did not believe other women to do, she did these queer things and did not always know why. The dirt would be all on her and stick tight, but she was not to mind it. She placed her hand over her brow and looked for shapes in the clouds in the sky, as she had done as a little girl.

The boys spotted Hester on the ground and came over to her. Aaron lay beside her. Lonnie squatted down and used her leg to rest his knees upon and kept balanced in his crouched stance. Steven paced around the handful of rows in the plot, near but not committed.

Hester pointed up to a cloud that appeared like a clump of cotton passing over.

"What does that look like to you?"

"I don't know," Aaron said, as he squinted to make out something other than a cloud.

"What do you think it looks like? It could be anything."

"I don't know," Aaron said again.

"I think it looks like a donkey in a bad mood," she told them. Hester heard Kip in her head say she shouldn't live so much in the dream world, but she went on with her game. "And that one over there is like a hare in a top hat."

Lonnie and Aaron laughed.

"And that one here, what's that?"

"I don't know," Aaron said for a third time. Then he added, "Children at school say that I'm stupid."

"They don't know what they are talking about," she said.

"Then why do they say it?"

Neither took their eyes from the clouds. Hester couldn't think of the words to say that wouldn't harm the boy. She impressed upon them the importance of honesty, and even though the truth was the truth, she couldn't speak it aloud.

"What does Mr. Evans say?" she found herself asking.

"He says Aaron is rare," Lonnie offered.

"You are irreplaceable to me." Hester nudged the boy with her elbow. "Does he say anything else?"

"That my heart is big like yours," Aaron told her.

Hearing that Kip spoke of her made a concave in Hester's chest, but she could not show that to anyone.

"Yes, you have a big heart, bigger than the state of Missouri," she said.

"That's impossible," Aaron replied with a laugh.

"Where did those horses come from?" Steven pointed to the two extra horses tied to the fence of the slowly developing pasture.

"They appeared here in the night," she told them.

"Are they orphans too?" Lonnie asked.

"In a way, but I don't suspect we can let them stay long," she said.

"Why not?" Aaron wanted to know.

"Jayhawkers, soldiers, ruffians, all come here searching for something they can't find," she told him. "And we have to keep it that way."

"What they lookin' for?" asked Lonnie.

"A reason to act."

"Does that mean we won't let Eben stay much longer?" Lonnie asked with concern.

"No, he will stay."

"What about Marlow?"

"He will stay too."

"Why them and not the horses?" Aaron wanted to know.

"You make exceptions for family."

"I liked it best when it was just the four of us," Aaron confessed.

"Even my brother is a little unsure of Marlow," said Steven. "He called him a wild card."

HESTER WALKED INTO THE KITCHEN and found Marlow pulling out china from a sack and arranging the dishes in the bare cabinet. She went and stood behind her brother.

"Marlow, where did you get this?"

"Don't mind where I got it." He didn't make eye contact with her. "Now we have more than enough for all of us."

Hester picked up one of the plates and held it in her hands. She ran her fingers across the painted flower pattern on the dish. She knew Marlow assumed that she was judging him from the moment he arrived, but he was a root of her and she cared for him just as deep whether he ate meat raw or not.

"I'd rather have nothing than something that created another loss," she said softly.

"Well, they aren't going to be needing it," Marlow told her.

A slight, sinister smile crept across her brother's face, and she tsked in disgust.

The next moment came from nowhere. Marlow grabbed the plate from Hester's hand and flung it across the room. They watched as it broke against the wall and dropped to the floor. Hester heard the wail before she realized it had come from her mouth. She was on the floor in front of a dead family's chosen china pattern, small pieces scooped in her hands. She knelt before the wreckage as one might kneel before a dying baby animal. Marlow threw another piece of the ivory-colored collection at the wall above her head and the pieces sprayed around her.

"If you don't want it," he said more than once, each time hurling another item from the bag. Hester stood up and blocked the flying china with her arms.

Marlow then pushed the table over. He growled at her. He grabbed for Hester's skirt. Hester moved a few steps away from him, but he continued his advance, knocking anything about that came within arm's length; he kicked at a chair, a pot cooling on the stove he swatted across the room with his palm. Hester barely had time to move away from each object. She kept saying her brother's name in hopes that he would hear her familiar sound.

Marlow got hold of her dress an inch below her waistline and gripped it tight and flung her across to the wall. Upon impact Hester's head snapped back and she slid down onto the floor, patches of black clouding her vision.

It had all happened so quick and suddenly the door was open, and someone was there. She looked up and a man she did not know had Marlow pinned against the wall, one arm braced across Marlow's chest, another cupped under Marlow's chin, squeezing his throat. She couldn't hear what the stranger was saying to her brother, but clearly they knew each other. She had never witnessed another control her brother before.

The stranger was very tall and lean, the way they depicted Lincoln in the papers. He had a distinct jawline that was clenched as he spoke the quiet words to her brother. She watched as Marlow's breath calmed, the dangerous anger lifting from his eyes. The man loosened his grip on Marlow's throat. They started to breathe together and finally the hand was removed from Marlow's throat altogether. The man rested it on Marlow's shoulder and gave it one squeeze, then stepped away from him.

Hester rose and walked out of the kitchen onto the back porch. A beautiful woman was in one of the chairs. This second stranger stroked a long braid that was draped over her shoulder as she stared unflinchingly at the open field. Then suddenly she turned away as if being released or letting go of a thought she had been holding on to tightly.

THIRTEEN

MARLOW

Aimee went around the house stringing bells to all the doorknobs. "To keep the spirits out," she said. Then she sent Royal and me out to the edge of the wood lookin' for a certain nettle to add to the stew she was making.

Royal says nothing about pullin' me from Hester at first. He talks of meeting up with Bushwhackers and learning that they are regrouping and will be headed our way. He says he passed by quite a few towns filled with Yankee soldiers and Jayhawkers searching for a fight and that our friends are planning to give them one.

"You come down the open road?" I ask Royal.

"My name's not known in these parts as yours is," he says.

"And your long hair?"

"Folks chalkin' it up to just being an eccentric foreigner, I suppose."

I know no man in these parts has long hair these days unless he is trying to prove something, and still, I believe if anyone could make every man look away, it's Royal. I think highly of Royal and he knows it is so.

"Why's she out of the woods?" I ask of Aimee.

"She came to see the sick Wendell boy, to read his future," he tells me.

"And the outcome? What'd she see?"

"Nothing, she didn't see a thing."

"Well, she doesn't sound very good at her magic."

"Perhaps it's as you say." Royal nods. "Perhaps there was nothing left to see."

He finds the tree we've been searching for and we start pulling.

"Interesting thing, you letting a Yankee tend to your house and sister," Royal says. "You did nothing about it, and the gang hear of all this, they'll kill you good and right."

"I haven't made up my mind about that yet. I might put a bullet in him still," I confess.

"What's stalling you?"

"I am waiting for a time when Hester will take more kindly to the idea."

"You want me to take care of it?"

"It's my business, I'll handle it," I promise.

"My knowing about it makes it my business now."

"I said, I'll deal with it my way."

"I will stand with you on this because I've seen you string the intestines of Unionists from one end of a town to another," says Royal. "I know you have no heart for Yankees, but you better not be going soft on the matter at hand. This better be because of your sister and no more."

Royal tells me I am picking the nettle wrong and damaging the tree, and corrects me.

"You got a funny way of showing your affection for you kin—trying to take a bite of her."

I say nothing.

"Where I am from, we have these low diving birds that have adapted so that they can plummet deep into the sea to make a catch. If they go too deep, they can't surface and will drown."

"Why you telling me this?"

"You must know how far your limits go, either way. A bird's got to know when enough is enough," he explains.

"I know my course."

"How deep are you going to dive, Marlow?"

I COME BACK TO THE house and offer all we found. Aimee crushes them down to dust in a clay bowl with other spices from the collection she brought along with her. The three orphans have gathered around her. Lonnie and Aaron have the chairs and Steven paces slowly around the kitchen, watching Aimee's movements. I rest the back of my head against the wall Royal had me pinned down but don't lean into it. Lonnie bends across the table on his elbows and peers into the bowl.

"What are you doing?" he asks.

"To add to supper," Aimee tells him. "Unwinds those wound too tight."

"Are you a witch of the deep woods?" Aaron asks on behalf of all the boys.

"I am."

Steven stops pacing. Lonnie swallows hard, then gains the courage to speak.

"Are you going to cut off our tongues and ears and hearts and cook them in a stew?"

"Only if you are very, very bad," she says, with a sly smile.

Aimee stops crushing the plants and focuses on each of the boys in turn.

She says to Aaron, "It's not that your momma didn't want you. You'll always be happier here and so in the end your Ma done right by you." To Lonnie she promises, "She won't die on you 'til she is old and white-haired and you are good and ready for it." Then she turns and examines Steven. "You get your mind right. Stop thinking what you're thinking."

"What do you mean by that?" Steven snaps.

"You know what I mean by it. You stop listening to what the dead tell you to do."

I expect her to turn to me, but she doesn't. I wait. Finally like she's hearing my impatience she says, "I am not ready for you yet. Go outside and play."

I AM SUPPOSED TO BE keeping an eye on the boys in the yard but instead I am asleep in Hester's shucking chair on the back porch. I am dreaming of battle. My mouth fills with that metallic taste I get before a fight, like sucking on a bullet. In the dream I have more arms, as if I am a human arachnid, holding both guns and knives in many hands. I am running through a field that at first appears like the field I am asleep in front of. I am the strongest warrior and my movements so graceful that men don't know where I come from or what weapon I will draw, and I cut them down like pigs on a slaughter line. In the dream I think how very similar it is to the dances I attended at the Hollisters' barn. Those who got there too late were always left without dance partners and if you timed it just so, you could move from one number to the next without a pause, without having to make awkward conversation with others left holding their rhythm. I can move through men. I cut men down.

I am awoken when a hand is placed on my shoulder. Without thought I dance this person onto the ground, with my knee holding down their stomach, one arm on their forehead, the other pressing across the chest bracing both arms. After a moment, I blink twice and see that it is Lonnie. The boy's face sickens with surprise. I pull myself off the boy and stand over him. He doesn't move, and I notice that a wet spot is forming on the porch between the boy's trouser legs. I extend my hand down to the child. The boy doesn't take it. He stands up on his own, bursts into tears.

"Why'd you do that?" he cries, fleeing the porch and running off into the field.

I THOUGHT ROYAL AND I would go out hunting after the darkness covered Missouri, but as supper ended, and all of us were still clustered in the kitchen with not enough space for all to sit, a fog began to fall over me. I couldn't keep my eyes open. I may have fallen asleep in the chair. Royal helped me up to my room and covered me with my blanket. Aimee comes to me in a dream. We are in the field behind the house. It is dark. There are no stars. No nature sounds. I can hardly see her, but I know she is there.

"Are you afraid, Marlow?" she asks. "You will have to account for your sins."

"I am not afraid," I tell her and I mean it.

"You should be."

I'M JILTED FROM A DEEP sleep by the sound of horses in the front yard and unfamiliar voices. The room is lit from a midday sun. I crawl over to the window and see several Jayhawkers spread out in the yard on horseback. I see Cody Brinson. He is leaning down and talking a casual tension with the orphan boys who are clumped together in the yard. Asking them their ages and where they come from. I reach for my guns and try and slither down the stairs without sound.

I put my back in the space between the door and the window. I see Royal sitting on a chair on the front porch. Aimee is using the sill of the window frame as a seat.

Cody addresses someone on the porch I can't see.

"You know there's a strong Confederate history in that house you've found yourself in."

I realize Eben must be placed somewhere near the porch steps.

"So you say," Eben responds.

"So we all say. So we all know for a fact," declares Cody. "There is more of a secesh presence in that house than in this whole state. Don't you got grudges you want to act on for what they did to your people in Kansas?"

"I'm all settled up," Eben tells him. "We won the war. That is the victory all the trouble was for and can now end. We have no quarrel with you, the children and I, let me take the boys into town, they can go to the schoolhouse where they can play with other children who also have no clash with you."

I hear his footsteps on the porch stairs and then the unmistakable sound of guns cocking.

"I've got a quarrel with the whole South and you're in the South when in this house," Cody warns.

"War's over," I hear Aaron say.

"War's just beginning," one of the other men in the yard calls out. "And even you will have to choose what side you're on."

"We will be on the side Hester tells us to be on," little Lonnie says, and I realize he has no idea of the magnitude of this moment because he's situated between his adopted brothers and knows they will protect him and that is a strength-giving knowledge.

"You need to make up your own mind," the man retorts.

"Is that what you did?" Eben says, taking a down step. "Or did you do what your father told you to do, like the rest of them?"

"I am tired of this conversation," Cody cuts in. "Where's Marlow?"

And like that I come from the house, guns stretched out in front of me. I turn slightly so Royal can see the dual pistols I have tucked in the back of my waist belt.

"Well here you are—out of hiding," Cody calls to me.

"I don't see anyone hiding," I tell him.

"You better put those guns away before someone gets hurt," Eben says to the men.

"There are a lot of us and only one gun hand on your side as I see it," says a man not from near here, naively.

Hester comes out then onto the porch and passes by me. She holds a cutting knife in her hand. The kind for gutting chickens. She holds it upward close to her side. The strongest way to hold a knife.

"Cody, I've known you my whole life. I know there is a heart in you somewhere, but if you don't start using it, I am going to come at you and cut it out."

This startles everyone, even me. I admit, I lower my guns a bit, but for just a moment. I can't see her expression, but I see Cody's glare at my sister.

"This shouldn't happen like this, we shouldn't shed blood in front of the children," someone says. It could have been anyone. Everyone holds. Finally Cody turns his horse away from us. He leers at me over his shoulder.

It is silently agreed upon and the intruders start to turn their horses toward town.

"This doesn't end it," Cody promises.

"No, it don't, not even an inch," I say.

Cody rides away without looking back. I know he will come for me.

"We better gather our things and head out," I say to Royal.

"No," Hester says, turning toward me.

"Be sensible, girl. They'll come back. It would be easier on you if we skid out."

She holds the cutting knife up to my stomach.

"No," she says again and goes on inside.

FOURTEEN

EBEN

Spring, 1866

In the room they shared Eben had tried to make a thick bedding out of leaves for him and Hester, which had worked out well in the army—kept him warm in the winter and cool in the summer months—but up in their room the leaves turned quickly and started to smell of the decomposing that accompanied death. Hester had asked him to throw them out. He scooped them a handful at a time from the window, to the delight of Aaron and Lonnie who stood underneath and laughed into hysterics as the clumps of leaves fell atop them. Eben and Hester went back to sleeping on the hard floor with only a few thin blankets between them and the wood. He could tell that her sleep had become even more restless these days, for her breath seemed cut short. He knew this was because of Marlow. Eben assumed Hester was fighting her brother off in her dreams. Marlow made her more nervous than any intruder. His nature was violent. Eben also knew that Hester defiantly loved her brother.

Hester came into the room and removed her clothing. She slipped on her nightdress and sat cross-legged in front of him at the end of their bed of quilts. Eben could hear Royal and Aimee stepping around in the room across from them that they'd moved into for a time. Marlow relocated to the first floor with the boys or to wherever he slunk to at night.

"Will it be like this much longer?" Hester asked.

"Like what?"

"As it is now?" She wanted him to be an oracle and tell her the future, but he did not have that power, though he wished he had everything to give her.

"It shouldn't be too long before things change again," he said.

"How so?"

"It could go this way or that," Eben told her.

"That could be said about all things."

"That threat of you not loving him anymore is not going to keep Marlow from shooting me."

"You don't know my brother. You don't know the weight of it." Hester crawled over to her side of the bed to lie down and Eben did the same.

"He wasn't like this before," she said. "He wasn't always so angry."

"He is in the darkness. War changes many men."

"How did it change you?"

"War took from me, ways I can't say aloud."

Eben knew Hester felt that same was true for her.

"Do you believe he will get better?" she asked.

"I have to believe that. So do you."

She reached over and started to undo the buttons of his nightshirt.

EBEN TRIED HIS BEST TO keep his distance from Marlow and Royal whenever possible. But there were times when there was no way around it. Sometimes he felt as though Marlow set the two of them up for confrontation.

"What is it?" Eben asked, coming upon Marlow in the hall. He had been waiting for him.

"I can't find my knife."

"Ask Steven, he may have seen it."

Marlow put his foot out, blocking Eben's path.

"Seems like you're comfortable taking what's obviously another's."

"Same could easily be said for you. Check with the boy. He may know who walked off with it."

"I always have another."

Eben kept his guard up and when he went anywhere alone, he took his revolver.

EBEN WAS FISHING AT THE creek with the boys when Aimee came to find him. She didn't need to look in the bucket to know the fish weren't biting. She pulled the neck of her coat tighter around her throat, held it closed and sat down on the log next to the man who no longer thought himself a soldier, but who still watched the tree line. The light blindingly flickered through the branches, and the birds chanted their sweet song.

"Perhaps," Aimee spoke. "You should return to that place you are from for some time."

Eben shook his head. "There is nothing there for me now. My place is here, though I am on an edge. Why doesn't your man try and kill me?"

"Royal is loyal to a person before any cause. Marlow says no, Royal will hold on it, even if the reason given may not be that good. You know what I mean—you got a girl exactly the same way."

He felt Aimee study his profile.

"You haven't asked me to read your palm," she said.

Eben kept his eyes on the boys.

"Nothing you can tell me I don't get to see for myself at some point."

"We all have moments where we can feel something coming, feel it so strong we actually see it. It sits somewhere in our gut and appears to us like a flash of light. I know you have felt it building, have that sense that something is coming."

"Then maybe I should be here to stop it," Eben said.

"Maybe you not being here will," she foretold.

"I wonder do you see your outcome as you can see others'?"

Aimee did not answer him. She stood and went over to Aaron and ruffled the bushy hair on top of his head, as if for luck, and then walked back toward the house.

THE NEXT DAY, THE MEN arrived.

"What's that sound?" Lonnie asked. They were collected around the first floor of the house, waiting out the end of a thunderstorm. The noise came from the woods, not the road.

"Riders!" Marlow said, and he and Royal shot up from their chairs to go to the windows at the back of the house.

"Who is it?" Hester asked.

"Looks friendly. I think it's Boston's men," Marlow said, scanning the field.

Then the adults considered Eben.

"You better get your man into hiding," Royal commanded. "They find him, we'll all pay for it. Every one of us."

Eben rose calmly and walked up the stairs to the second floor. Marlow and Royal went onto the porch to welcome their comrades.

After the greetings had been done and the Bushwhackers began to make camp in the yard, those that knew what was hid inside the house gathered in Hester and Eben's upstairs room.

"They will stay no more than two, three days. Can you sit tight 'til then?" Royal asked Eben.

Eben knew it wasn't a true question for him to answer, no one here would follow his lead. He found he wasn't as worried about his own safety, as he was anxious the men's presence would alter the routine they had established for the boys. He believed that consistency was what the boys needed and desired for themselves.

"What if someone comes and searches the house?" Steven asked.

"Then we'll have something new to worry about," Marlow replied.

"Is there anyone you trust that could keep him until they move on?" questioned Royal.

"Hester is the only one taking in strays these days," Marlow said.

"There is no one you trust?" Aimee asked.

"Kip." Hester heard herself say it before she realized the name was creeping up her throat. "Take him to Kip's."

"I don't believe that's good accord," Marlow said.

"Can you trust this man?" Royal asked.

"Yes, we can trust him," Marlow confirmed.

"The next time the group moves," Royal decided for them. "You stay behind and bring Hester's man about."

"Why should I trust you?" Eben asked Royal.

"What choice you see yourself having?"

EBEN ORGANIZED HIS TRAVELING GEAR in the knapsack he had put away and not brought out in many months until that night. He heard the men in the yard, at least a handful of different voices, but he knew there were probably more. He went to the bed and began to roll up one of the blankets the way he had done in the war when they were told they would be moving out. Marlow and Royal came into the room and watched how Eben arranged his sack. They all had their own way of doing this and, after years of it, memorized the order for which they placed their belongings inside a pack.

Marlow flicked a few coins down onto the floor in front of Eben, both Union and Confederate.

"In case you get in a jam or decide it's better you head out," Marlow told him. Eben knew making eye contact with Marlow was always a risk, so he kept his eyes focused on his pack.

"Confederate money won't be took at any store around here now and they don't want me in town any which way."

"Curious as to why not," says Royal.

"On account I fought for the Union," said Eben, without missing a beat, not recognizing Royal's words as sarcasm.

"Aw now, it's probably on account you're living in sin with Marlow's sister."

Eben glanced up, startled by the accusation, and saw

112

that Royal was smiling subtly. It occurred to Eben that the man had been making a small joke.

"I suppose it could be that."

"Well, if it's not one thing, then it's another," Royal said. As Royal and Marlow left the room, Royal put his hand on the back of Marlow's shoulder, steering him like a colt.

HESTER MET EBEN ON THE stairs as he came down from the room after darkness had fallen. The Bushwhackers had left for their hunt and he was to set out in the company of Marlow. It was agreed Aimee would go along to supervise the transaction, acting as a buffer between the men.

Hester looked forlorn. He hated seeing her that way. It reminded him of when they first met.

"I do not want to die alone," Hester confessed to Eben. "For that time I was by myself in this house, when I had to shoot the horse, I thought this is the end of the world, and there is no one else, this is how it will conclude. Then it didn't. It went on and on. Then the boys came, and I had to survive not only to see what happened next but so that they could. Then you came and I started to see what it was like to do more than wait and survive. Now we're going backward and—"

"I know you are fearful I am leaving, that I can walk away from our life here. That if we are in Purgatory I will cross without you," Eben cut in. "But I will not. I am going so that our life here can continue, that is what I want most."

"You are leaving me in the house of crazy," she said.

What Hester didn't know was that during those midnight make-sures all those months ago when he first arrived, when she appeared on the stairs to check on the children, the little noise of her presence on the steps and the extra light of the candle woke Eben. He would see her aglow on the other side of the room and feel like a boatman that had just seen shore. Eben did something then that surprised them both. He stepped down and put his lips on hers. She put her hands on the sides of his face and they embraced openly on the staircase.

WHEN MARLOW BROUGHT EBEN UP to Kip's cabin, Eben inspected the headmaster cautiously, as Kip peered through the cracked-open doorway at the two men and the woman cloaked in the night's shade. The teacher seemed smaller of a man than he did when he was on the steps of the schoolhouse, or when he had stood up for Eben to the shopkeeper before the New Year.

"Hester said you'd look after Eben 'til the rangers continue on. You in good health with this?" Marlow asked his old friend. "I think it's as queer as a no-legged-rooster, but we got no one else."

"He can't stay here," Kip said.

"He's got to stay here, or I got to kill him, we got men on our plot," Marlow insisted. Eben recoiled only slightly at the mention of his death.

"I said, he can't stay here. I have Union officials watching me close, making sure I don't teach any Southern pride in the schoolhouse, and the townspeople watch me because they want to be sure I am still true to them. If I am seen being social with either you or the Unionist I'll be turned against."

Marlow didn't listen.

"If you run out of subjects to talk on, you can always fall back on the topic of Hester. Though that might not be the most proper conversation, be theatre to witness."

"It will all work itself out fine," Aimee coaxed.

"Or one of you might go ahead and kill the other in their sleep," Marlow said, and slicked his hair back with his palm.

"I am not going to stay here if he isn't willing to have me. Certainly not if things look this bad on the way in," Eben said, turning away from the house.

"I said you are staying here," Marlow commanded. And as Eben turned to look over his shoulder, he was hit in the face with the butt of Marlow's pistol, and everything went dark and cold.

EBEN WOKE INSIDE THE SCHOOLTEACHER'S home tied to a chair, arms and legs bound.

"What is this?" Eben asked, and struggled to move against the bonds.

"We thought this would be best for now," Kip said, hovering over the kettle on the stove. "Well, Marlow thought it best."

"Where's Marlow and Aimee?"

"They left," Kip told. "Aimee wanted me to tell you not to worry. I don't have it in me."

"Is that her promise, or yours?"

"Both of ours," Kip said weakly. "I am not going to strangle you with my one arm."

"No, but you may pick up that rifle and go at me with it."

"I won't need to do that as long as you keep yourself planted in that chair until they come get you."

"That could be days."

"It better not be days."

All Eben had to do was turn them all in to the military with a sweep of the hand. If not for the reaction of Hester, he knew that he would have done so already.

"It's only a little funny," Eben said to himself. "But still there is some humor in it."

"What are you saying?"

"I fought in the war for many years, battle after battle, but it wasn't until coming to this town that I started to feel like I have truly had an awful lot of close calls, ones I saw laid out right in front of me."

Eben had an itch on his nose that he couldn't scratch. He jerked his head trying to shake it off. The jolt ignited the pain in his forehead from the pistol butt. Kip sat down at his eating table and so he was facing Eben centered in the middle of the room.

"We don't need to talk no more," Eben said.

"You got something else to do?"

"Why'd you have Marlow tie me up before he'd gone?"

"Because you are a soldier and because I am a soldier."

"The war is over for me. Now I am just a man you got tied to a chair."

"The war will never truly be over, nothing will ever be as we want it here." Eben could hear in the man's voice that he had not spoken about the war much since he left the battlefields and that it was hard for him to do so. His face was contorted in confusion and sadness.

"People talk like that a lot here," Eben observed. "That isn't a way of living."

"If you haven't noticed, we are the ones that lost the war."

"It doesn't have to be the end all," Eben counseled.

"We have to just wait until you tell us what to do next, how else you want us to change our way of being."

"Seems like it's Marlow calling the shots right now in both our cases," Eben said. He twisted his wrists against the rope. "It wouldn't take all that much for me to get out of these binds," he confessed.

"If you mean what you say of being no harm, you won't try to get out."

"That's strange logic."

"It would be foolish of me to take Marlow's word on anything," Kip said. "He doesn't see things exactly as they are."

"Well, now we agree on something," Eben said. "What about Hester? What does her word mean to you?"

"We don't need to talk anymore," Kip said. "You sleep quiet in that chair tonight, in the morning I promise I'll release you."

CHAPTER

FIFTEEN

MARLOW

The raiders make camp in the field behind the house as if it were nothin' and no trouble. There is a dampness left from the continual rain that has ceased and allowed the sun's sporadic burns to shine. The heat is rising and the first sprouts have appeared, risking a last-chance snow. The brief hidden smell of lilac that blows on the wind for days has left me looking out ahead.

We had all rode together with Quantrill and then we split off with Patsy Boston when Quantrill went south and then we split off again when Boston wanted to go after Kentucky. At the time Royal and I hadn't felt like suicide, but as it turned out it wasn't that at all and they left the county with a bucketful of gold and quite a few scalps.

The dozen Bushwhackers lounged around in the field, relaxing as though Jayhawkers couldn't come upon them at any time. They dried their clothes on the line, played checkers. In other times, and with more women, this day would have appeared like a picnic. A few of us gather on logs around the fire pit and roast one of Hester's chickens. Mr. Jeremy has come from town to join us. Our discussion is of surrenders and revenge, although it could seem like any other gathering outside in the first days of spring.

"Surrender may be dandy for those deep South, those cotton-picks and swampies," explains Boston, the gruff, bloodletting militant. "But I go into Jefferson City revolver-less, they're going to take one look at my face and someone's kin that I've sent to the ferryman is going to recognize it and do me in right there, same goes for you lot." Boston singles out several of the fighting men, including me, in his gesture. Then he points over to Royal, who has taken a keen interest in his horse this day, brushing it down, seeing to its shoes, not committing to the war talk. Royal regards Boston with just a turn of the head but then goes on with his business. Royal had once told me that his ancestors had prepared their horses for battle as if the horses were soldiers themselves. Royal and Boston had an old tradition of war in them. They revered one another for it.

"All but him," Boston says about Royal. "No one seems to know his face. He has God on his side."

Royal never put much weight in God. He believes you got demons inside you, you got saviors, they shine through, what you are is them, you fight them, you do as they say or you don't, you make these choices, not no god. God's the one that put all them there to see what you'd do. God likes to test and tease.

"How long are you going to keep running?" Mr. Jeremy asks the men.

"We ain't runnin," Decker says in the tone of someone who has just been insulted. "We're strategizing." From the moment he arrived at our plot I could tell Decker was not the same straight shot I'd known before I crossed the Tired Dog River and came home. He'd taken to keeping a bottle of bark juice to his lips when he wasn't using them like a snapping turtle.

"He's right, we're getting ready for our last stand," Boston assures us.

"That's what we said back in Lawrence and it's been a long time since then. Nothings changin," Ludlow says under his breath, but we all hear. He was the youngest of the Bushwhackers, joined up the same age Steven is now. Even though he's been fighting as long as any of us, he's still a kid to the oldest fighters among us.

"Boy, the attitude toward a fight you were lucky to get out of appalls me and makes me melancholy," Boston tells him scornfully. "You speak like that, and you are on your way to the lost." Boston knew a thing or two of the way of the lost, having watched many of his kin be taken from this earth, but he carried forth and brought two handfuls of men along with him.

"Perhaps if we had gone east like the others when we first heard of the deal," Ludlow says, meaning what Ulysses

Todd and the Leroy Gang had done. "Maybe we would all be home now, living under Yankee law, but living clean instead of being here, smelling of hogs in a pit."

The bullet goes through Ludlow's head as the period rests at the end of his sentence. Blood arranges itself on Ludlow's neighbors. Mr. Jeremy stumbles back off his log and rubs at the blood on him, trying to assure himself it is not his own. Boston does not move. He lets out a long exhale. He doesn't even consider the blood on him. I know the men won't say boo because they understand why I have removed Ludlow from the conversation, but I share it aloud because Hester has come out of the house at the shot and she no longer always hears everything I say inside myself.

"I am not interested in living under anyone else's laws but my own," I say. I've known this boy for years, but it was easier to kill him than it's been to kill the Union soldier in my own home. That is the power Hester still has on me.

I holster the pistol and pick up Ludlow under the armpits and start to drag him across the field. Royal comes over and takes the dead man's legs and together we bring him out past the property line and bury him in a low grave.

I DO NOT LIKE THE unorganized nature of our presence, which has been our way for some time now since Quantrill is no longer our leader and Bloody Bill is gone. We still send out scouts as we move through the dusk looking for

Jayhawkers or military, or those that have crossed us in bad accord, but we are sloppy in our cover-up, Boston letting the men do as they choose.

Tempting was Texas territory, where rebels roamed with abundance, where finders keepers. But there is no Hester in Texas and until there is, I will not cross over the southwest corner of Missouri.

Back when I was in a jam not far from Pilot Knob, I lay with my back against the small hill and I promised that if I got out of that one, the fates could do whatever they wanted with me. I'd offer them anything, except Hester, if I got out of that desperate ditch unharmed. As the men fell around me, I knew I would give it all, except Hester, except her. And I did make it out and a week later Pa was killed. I am sure that I traded his life for my own.

I have nothing left to offer now, but the one thing I never will.

We are entering the next county on some sorry one-way path when we come to a group of soldiers, diehard Zouaves, in their poof and swagger. We should have seen the signs that we were reaching a camp, but we come across them by chance and them upon us with even more bad luck.

Royal dismounts from his horse and charges at a Zouaves on his own two legs which is not what we are expectin' but then neither are they. We all watch as Royal reaches the nearest man, grabs hold of the hair on the back of his head and smashes the baffled soldier up against a nearby pine. His nose is crushed into his skull and if he doesn't die of his injury, it is the kind of damage he'll wish he had. Royal lets go of his hair and the man crumples to the ground. No amount of their fancy training has readied them for combat with Royal. By this time the band of soldiers is coming to terms with what is taking place. Royal moves to the next man and pulls his Arkansas toothpick on him. This greenhorn has enough instinct to pull his Colt from his waist, but there isn't time, and Royal is on him, cutting his throat and relieving him of his pistol. I will not lie; his movements awe me. Awe us all. Royal takes out another man simultaneously shooting him with his comrade's weapon on the right side of his stomach and stabbing him with the knife in the left.

The rest of us join the fight. I take my shot at a Zu-Zu on horseback and hit him in the leg. He shoots back in my direction but the pain in the leg is a distraction and he misses, which is his misfortune because when he reaches down to clutch at his leg, I am still here and shoot him through the ribs.

It takes all but two minutes. Most of us never leave our horses.

"What a thing of beauty," Boston says, watching Royal. Drenched in the blood of these men, as if he had been swimming in their insides, he goes to each body and cuts the throats of those that failed to die in his first assault. When time permitted, Royal never left a battle without being sure each man down had made it across the threshold and was with their maker. He left no man waiting.

CHAPTER

SIXTEEN

LONNIE

"Who are you?" Boston asked the little boy peering through the open slits in the man's small tent he hung between two bur oaks.

"Lonnie."

Boston had his many guns laid before him and he was cleaning each one with the same delicate care as Marlow did with his. Lonnie had no interest in guns.

Boston pointed to Hester, who stood across the field in conversation with her brother. "Who's that beautiful and strong woman to you?"

"That's my mother," Lonnie said.

"She seems a bit young to be your Ma."

"Eben says she would be if I let her, so I'm lettin' her," Lonnie told him.

"And who is Eben?"

"I am lettin' him be my Pa," said the little boy.

"Where is this man you're letting be your Pa?"

"He's gone right now," Lonnie said.

"Son, anyone gone right now isn't ever coming back."

"You're gone from somewhere," Lonnie observed.

"And I ain't ever coming back from this," Boston told him.

CHAPTER

SEVENTEEN

HESTER

Before the war, when there was talk of war, and then when there was unsanctioned action, there'd be meetings at the Cain house, meetings other women didn't want in their homes so they told their men to go elsewhere. Hester had been too young to tell her Pa that such talk should be kept for woods and for prayers in church, so these groups of men occasionally congregated at their home and Hester served tea and shortbread, because there was still some manners then. She had known this war a long time. There wasn't any looking away from it.

Now the Bushwhackers gathered again, but they were not hiding. Men on both sides of the war had gotten out of the habit of asking permission for anything. There was no way to move them along and Hester had to admit to herself that if she had anything she could offer them, she would give it, for this is the role they dealt her and it was better than none at all, better than being ignored, and better than a bullet.

LATE IN THE DAY, WHEN many of Marlow's comrades still slept in their makeshift tents and under the shade of trees, Hester carried a bucket of well water toward the house. Lonnie and Aaron burdened the weight of another bucket together beside her. Faintly Hester could hear the sound of her brother humming, but she could not place him when she glanced around the yard.

Patsy Boston confronted the boys as they passed near the partially finished corral that was more of a hitching post with the row of horses tied to the beams. He took the bucket from the children effortlessly and held out a piece of rusted copper to Lonnie.

"I'll give you a Confederate coin to brush down my horse," he said to the boy.

Hester watched as Aaron grabbed Lonnie's hand and started to pull him toward the house.

"Where you going?" Boston called.

"Hester would want me to say that you can't have him for your Cause," Aaron shouted back and tugged Lonnie along.

"It's just a coin," Boston promised.

"No, it's not just a coin," Aaron hollered. "No, no, no, that's not all it means."

Hester watched as Aaron forced Lonnie through the back door of the house and then closed the door behind him.

"That boy isn't right in the head," Boston said as he came up and relieved Hester of her bucket as well.

"Perhaps not but the war broke many."

"Not you it seems."

"You would be incorrect to say so," Hester said.

They walked together toward the house.

"You know, when your brother was free with his words, and they weren't of talk about warrin', they were of you. The way he spoke, I assumed you'd be meek," he told her. "Frail and breakable. And you, miss, certainly are not." Hester was not surprised to hear her brother had spoken of her, speaking of one another always made them feel closer to each other. But had he thought her weak, he would not have left her alone all these years.

"Had we more like you, perhaps we would have won this war long ago," Boston said. Hester wondered if it was really the compliment it was meant to be.

"It was always easier to have Marlow do the fighting for me," she told him. "My whole life, Marlow would take care of what needed to be done. When he left to fight the war, that changed. I had to learn to survive without him. It has been very hard." Hester surprised herself with her honesty.

They reached the porch of the house and Hester could see Aaron watching through the window.

"Hester, you lose your man in this war?"

"Yes," Hester said, because she felt it to be so.

"You got another man now?" Boston asked her.

"I got more men than I know what to do with."

IN THE KITCHEN, AIMEE AND Royal sat with their chairs pushed close together. Royal rubbed Aimee's back in small circles and he was speaking softly to her. They broke apart when Hester came upon them. Aimee had begun to have dark crescents under her eyes in the last few days, as if she never slept. She was weaker than when she first arrived on their plot. Being around so many, with all their rugged pasts and impulse-changing futures, reading them had worn on her. Hester saw her molting the way birds in cages did.

"The Jayhawker Brinson, your Yankee man hunkered down with that Confederate schoolteacher, the men outside with all their questions, not to mention those three queer boys of yours," Royal says. "It seems as if we have everyone to worry about."

Hester rinsed her hands in a tub of water and dried them with a towel.

"Don't forget my brother, who watches every moment the way a wolf-dog studies a lamb."

"Is that so?" Marlow said, appearing in the doorway that led to the front room of the house. He leaned his back against the wood frame. "A wolf-dog am I now?"

Hester sighed and shook her head.

"Don't pretend you aren't picking a fight with every gesture," Hester said.

"We all must watch our backs from every angle," explained Royal.

"You're starting to become jagged," Marlow told his sister. He examined his hands. "I think you have lost that spark of righteousness you used to carry around. Perhaps that is why some connections have been severed and are not embraced as they once were."

Hester knew that he was referring to Kip, though he could as easily be speaking of the link between the two of them. The trunk might be missing, but the roots were still in the ground.

"The only things I have lost is what the war took," Hester told him.

Royal cut in. "One of the first things Quantrill ever said to me was that we have made choices that will never allow for us to return to how it has been before, that we must move forward and press a future that is stronger than our past."

"I don't suspect taking up with Yankees is what he had in mind," Marlow said.

"They say Quantrill ate hearts," Hester coaxed.

"Yes, but don't we all in our own way?" said Royal, without any hint of emotion or afterthought.

"You cannot go backward, Hester," Marlow reminded her.

"I know that."

"Know it and mean it."

Hester had gone inside the chicken coop to collect eggs, but instead sat on the scat-filled ground, which she paid no mind. Legs crossed, hen in lap, Aimee found her there, stroking the feathers back.

"They often talk as if they are never going to let this war end, but history shows us it has to stop sometime," Aimee said, as she squatted down across from Hester. "People got to breathe again." The chicken in the nest behind her pecked some at her hair. She reached up and gently swatted it away.

Hester could not remember a time she had a confidant in another woman. She had played with other girls growing up, but they always felt she had the upper hand, for she was most often in the company of boys and of men, and that made other girls cautious of her. She found Aimee to be strong-willed, steadfast. Hester did not at all mind feeling like she was here to learn from her, that Aimee had things to teach her about herself. She thought all friendships should have that component, not just friendships with witches.

"I knew a woman who had eleven children and every single one of them died," Aimee told her. "After they were all gone, she had one more, a baby girl, and that girl had unique skills because she was a last hope."

"Why you telling me this?"

"By the cards I shouldn't be here, but here I am, as are you. We make do with what we have."

"You got a letting-go spell?" Hester asked.

"Oh, honey, there is no magic powerful enough for that. Time and work are what straightens that path."

"What kind of work?"

"The moving-forward kind. You are on the right course, you just keep doing what you're doing." They could hear the voices of men chatting off in the field, but it was just the two of them alone in the coop.

"I'm not doing anything."

"You keep good company. You're building up a new future. How can that be anything but the true course?"

"Can your magic protect someone?"

"You and Marlow, always wanting magic to do work you could probably do yourselves."

"Well, can it?"

"You cannot ask too much of the spirits, you must know exactly what you want, and when you're asking you must be specific and clear. Most importantly, you must be willing to accept your fate."

Aimee pulled from the pouch that hung from her hip, a well-used yellow candle. In front of her, she placed three small stones in three corners a foot apart symbolizing the directions. Aimee being a rock for the south. She then lit the candle. Hester and the chickens watched curiously.

"What is it you want to protect?" Aimee asked her.

Marlow was kin, he would give his life for Hester's without hesitation, even after being apart, he understood her like no other, and there was weight in that. Hester focused on the small flame and spoke to it.

"Keep Marlow from harm," Hester said.

"Your one wish and that is what you want?" Aimee questioned.

"That is enough for me."

"That was once enough for you, but is it enough for you now?"

Hester was conflicted by the loss of pride she felt in Marlow, and yet, she had to be true to him. He was her blood, because of that, he deserved more than anyone else she cared for.

"Marlow must not be harmed."

"There are many forms of pain, you know that well enough, Hester. Speak it right."

"Marlow must live and not die. Our lives are woven together so tightly. I cannot be broken from him, not for anything."

Aimee ran her hand over the flame and it went out. She started to gather the stones.

"Is that it?" Hester questioned.

"You were expecting something more?" Aimee asked her, amused.

"Did it work?"

"We shall see, that was an awfully big ask," Aimee told her.

"I know," Hester said.

Hester followed Aimee from the coop.

"I am tired of this land," Aimee told her. "I miss the sea."

"Why don't you go there now that the roads are open?"

"I love the ocean, it's inside my skin, but it's not my home, he is—" Aimee gestured over to Royal who was playing cards with a group of Confederates by a pup tent. "If I am not here to keep him balanced, no telling how he'd sway."

BOSTON CAME INTO THE KITCHEN—he held his hat in his hands as he stood before Hester.

"We will be breaking camp tomorrow," Boston told her.

"Where will you go?"

"Wherever the fight is."

"You cannot take Marlow."

"He said you'd say that."

"Well, you can't have him."

"He and Jamarquis will ride with us as far as the next county, see us off proper, then turn back." Boston hesitated, weighing his thoughts. "I don't think we will meet again," he finally spoke.

"Never has not happened just yet."

"If in another life we meet, I shall not hesitate to marry you," Boston told her with an air of certainty.

"If only all men could be as bold as you when it comes to the true nature of their hearts," wished Hester.

"In my favor they are not. I imagine I would have to wait in a long line for a woman such as yourself," Boston replied.

Hester considered going over to Boston and giving him a kiss, something soft and gentle, one that wished him luck and said goodbye as well, but after a moment she turned away and he left the house. It was not him who she wished to give such a kiss to, out of habit it was Kip, as it had always been. It made her angry at herself that he was her first thought, that she still wanted this, because he did not desire it, nor deserve it.

HESTER AND THE BOYS SAT close to the fireplace. After she finished reading aloud to them, Hester laid the book down on her lap. Lonnie got up, went to the couch and lay down, locking his hands behind his head and resting on them. It reminded Hester of how Eben did this, and it triggered an instant desire to be able to lie beside Eben, and rest her head on his arm.

"How much longer 'til those men leave?" Aaron asked.

"A few hours more," Hester told him.

"They are here to protect us," Steven said.

"Is that you talking or your brother?" Hester asked.

"My brother," he told her.

"You tell him they would probably get us all killed if they stayed. But how is this new to us? We will be just as bad off when they leave as when they came." Hester knew she shouldn't say such words to children, but she said it anyway.

"My brother said when they leave, I should go with them and fight."

"Over my dead body." Hester paused. "Over his."

CHAPTER

EIGHTEEN

EBEN

Eben had not slept while tied upright to the chair at Kip's cabin. When he started to nod off, he would wake himself when his head jerked forward or back. He knew that the schoolteacher slept little as well. In the night Eben would sometimes see Kip's irises' glow from catching the light and he could see the man watching him like a cautious raccoon.

In the morning Kip cut the rope that held down one of Eben's wrists. Eben's legs had become weak and he could not move his feet without losing balance. Kip was out the door and to the schoolhouse before Eben was able to make it on two feet.

After a restless morning cooped up alone in the house, Eben went out the back door and snuck around to the side of the schoolhouse where he could sit on the small slope and watch Hester's boys through the windows. He could not find Steven, but Lonnie and Aaron were there, sitting together in one of the rows. He wanted them to look out and see him so that he could wave, but he didn't want to be a distraction. He did not wish to be more of a burden on the schoolteacher then he knew he already was. He worried about Hester. He felt they lived with no roof but were surrounded by hundreds of walls.

Midday, the students in the schoolhouse were released outside for a break. Some of the children that lived in town returned home for a quick meal while others sat down around the yard and pulled tins from their satchels. Lonnie and Aaron saw Eben and they went up to him.

"Those men still at the house?" Eben asked the boys.

The boys nodded.

"What will you do if they stay a long time?" Lonnie asked.

"They won't."

"How do you know that?" Aaron said.

"Because they just can't. Where is Steven?"

"With the men," Lonnie told him.

"Well, tell him how much fun he missed at school today so that he will want to come tomorrow."

"But it isn't fun," Aaron said.

"It will be tomorrow," Eben lied.

"Steven says you shouldn't come back," Lonnie confessed. "That you don't belong with us."

"Steven doesn't know what is best for everyone."

"Steven's brother says, that if we want to live free, we have to live free of the Union," Lonnie recited, as if saying a memorized speech.

"Are you talking to Steven's brother now too?"

"Steven tells us what he says," Aaron admitted.

"Do you know what he means by that, by freedom?"

The boys shake their heads.

"You are already free," Eben told them. "Every living man holds equal weight to the next. You can be anything you work to become." He said this for his benefit, as much as the boys', a reminder of what he so confidently once believed. "Steven may tell you next that we are to enslave those who are not like us, those darker-skinned than us, those with different ways of life. Do you think that sounds fair and kind?"

"But shouldn't we be able to live any way we want?" Lonnie asked. "Steven says the Union is trying to take away our right to do that."

"You can live your life any way you please, as long as it doesn't chain another to you who does not want to be there." As soon as he said it, Eben knew this could be argued for the South's plight from the North. He could also tell the boys were going to continue to ask him questions why, and knew it was more than he could explain in the middle of the schoolyard. It might take many years for them to understand all the things this war had been fought over. "Run along now. I will talk to you again after school is finished for the day."

Lonnie and Aaron walked away from Eben and they went and ate with the other children.

Eben went up to the one-room building, stood in the doorway, and watched Kip, whose back was to him, struggle to try and hang the chalkboard that had come loose and fallen from the wall. He was unable to hold the nail in place and bring the hammer down at the same time, while also trying to prop the heavy board up in position with just his knee.

After a few minutes of awkward attempts, Kip stepped back in defeat.

"It must be very frustrating, going to do something you used to do easily, but finding it more of a burden now," Eben said, moving down the row of benches.

Kip turned to face him.

"Yes, it is indeed."

Both men were tired and it showed on them.

"I would be willing to help you with projects at the school, like this one here, things that could be done easily with three hands, more so than with just one."

"I suppose that would do," Kip agreed.

Eben came up to the front of the room.

"If you hold the frame up, I shall do the hammering," Eben offered.

Kip relinquished the tool to Eben and picked up the chalkboard with his one hand and held it propped against the wall with his body.

"Why would you help me?"

"This situation is about something bigger than the two of us."

"I can tell by the way the boys speak you are someone who believes in an academic education," Kip said.

"I do. Although I protested a good deal when I was their age, my mother saw to it that I spent a large amount of my youth learning all I could from books and those more educated than myself," Eben told him. "And I am the better for it. It has allowed me to see the linkage of many things. It has also helped me to understand people's emotions, instead of forcing an opinion of their actions."

Eben put a few nails up to his mouth and held them in his teeth. He moved around the frame of the chalkboard, hammering one nail after another into the wood to keep the board tight against the wall.

"Not too many mothers would be pleased to have their son, whom they had spent so much time raising to be lev-el-headed, be stuck in the predicament you have found yourself in," Kip said.

"And which predicament are you referring to exactly?"

"Oh, you can take your pick."

"Yes, well, my mother was killed in Lawrence, so I don't think she will say much on the subject."

"During the raid?"

"No, some time after that. Union men burned her house down because they said she was a Southern sympathizer. She ran back into the house to try and save all the animals she was caring for at the time and the smoke caught up to her. My mother would take in any living thing needing extra care. She would let freed slaves salvage what they could from her pantry. She helped birth babies. She tried to find husbands and wives for anyone, didn't mind what their stance on the war was or if they were bad looking, my mama just liked being helpful. They took that from her, and they took her from me."

Eben shook his head, blinked a few times. He had to hold back tears anytime he talked about his mother aloud for too long. If Kip still had his other arm, Eben sensed the schoolteacher might have rested a hand on his shoulder. The men stood back and observed their achieved task.

"Perhaps if those men had been properly taught to appreciate kindness, they would not have been hasty to punish an old woman," Eben added.

"You are still a dreamer then, even in a land of patriots," Kip said.

"I just believe in working your mind as hard as your body."

"There are a few more things I could use your help with," Kip said. "That is to say, if you'd trust me standing below you on a ladder."

"I'd be willing to go on your word the ladder will stay upright."

Kip led the way out behind the schoolhouse where the roof of the outhouse had caved in. The past was thick with thorns, but that does not prevent appreciation from growing. They had mutual interests in mind, and that did not require friendship.

LATE IN THE AFTERNOON AIMEE walked into town alone to fetch the boys. She approached Eben outside the schoolhouse.

There were townsfolk collected in small groups to talk of the day, and Eben could feel their gazes on them, could sense his name and the headmaster's were on people's lips.

"How are things at the house?" Eben asked her.

"She is fine," Aimee told him. "I am glad to see you are still with us."

"It was not nothing, as you foretold it would be."

"That is not what I said, but it wasn't anything you couldn't handle."

"You look dog-eared," Eben observed. "Are you ill?"

"I am living many lives right now; it does take its toll."

Cody Brinson and a few of his comrades rode into town on their horses. They made an announcement of their arrival by keeping their horses in gallop until they reached the town square. Turning up dust and wind on those outdoors. Cody saw Eben and Aimee and broke away from his group to come toward them.

"What have we here?" Cody asked. "The witch and the supposed soldier from Kansas. Some of Mr. Douglas' and Mr. Harris' sheep just went and fell over dead in the night. You wouldn't know anything about that, would you?"

"Why would we know anything about that?" Aimee asked.

"Being a witch, if you didn't spell them yourself, I'd think you'd be able to use your powers to tell me who did."

"No one did anything," Aimee told him.

"Is that so?" Cody walked his horse so close to Aimee that it nuzzled its head against her shoulder. "What are the chances of two men's animals dropping dead at the exact same time?"

"Their pastures wouldn't by chance be right next to one another?" Eben asked. Cody didn't respond. "It happens. When fences are too close, the animals keep passing illness back and forth, it's no one's fault."

"I will say when someone's at fault or when there's no fault," Cody said.

"You can say whatever you want," Aimee explained. "You will die a young death, and nothing shall change that outcome."

"You watch what you say, woman. I will have no problem burning the devil from you." Cody snarled and turned to Eben. "Or cutting the throat of a Copperhead."

Cody walked his horse backward. The horse's head and tail rose, twitching in a prancing gesture. Then Cody lodged his heels into the horse's hind, breaking the horse into a canter across town, back to his group of Jayhawkers.

Kip brought Aaron and Lonnie over to Eben and Aimee.

"How long will he play out as law of this town?" Eben wondered.

"Not much longer," Aimee told him.

"Cody is nothing but trouble," Kip said. "He's just sucking up air. He should never have been brought into this world."

"Don't do that," Aimee snapped at him. "Don't judge a man back to a time before he had yet proven himself to be what he is. You think you're something special, but you're not."

"Why would you say that? You don't even know me."

"I say it because no one else will. I don't need to know you. I know how people regard you or disregard you. That's all I need know."

Aimee took Aaron's hand and started to lead him down the road, away from town. Eben and Lonnie quickly followed, catching up to them. Aaron and Lonnie pushed on ahead, while Eben walked with Aimee. Her pace was weary.

"A calm normality is sure to come, but in slow and steady ways," Aimee assured Eben. "Yet, like the split of the landmasses, the breakaway will be painful and lasting."

"You put the coming as a riddle because you know it

would be impossible for a person to hear such truths as they really are."

"I say it to you thus because you do not ask me to put it any other way."

"If I walk away, what will happen?" Eben asked, though he knew he would never want to, even if he could.

"Villains will take from those you love," she said.

"And if I stay?"

"Villains will take from the loves of others."

Eben walked them to the edge of the town and then circled back to Kip's house.

EBEN LAY HIS MAT ON the floor for the night. Being that the cabin was small, he and Kip were no more than five feet from one another. Although no one was outside after dark, the town did not seem as quiet as Hester's home, situated around the cove of trees.

"Were you at Shiloh?" Kip asked in the dark.

"I believe I was over at Fort Pulaski at the time," Eben said.

"That was the worst one for me," Kip told him. "By then, I was just working the surgeon's tent as a physician's assistant. Saw men's bodies in ways they aren't ever supposed to be."

"A fight like that is a nasty thing," Eben confirmed.

"Do you dream about them?" Kip asked him.

"I do, but not as often as I once did."

"Same here. I think if I see you on the battlefield, even in a dream, I will be unable to shoot."

"I am much obliged."

"But Marlow, he won't hesitate to cut you down. If it wasn't for Hester, he would have already done so."

"If not for Hester, a lot of things," Eben said. "What do you reckon it is about those two siblings makes them so forgiving, and so willing to go against their gut for one another?"

"Oh, I always tried not to think too hard on it," Kip told him. "Gives me an unsettled feeling, all that attention they bestow on one another. I don't know no other siblings close as them."

"I think on it with wonder. Their influence is so strong. They can balance and unbalance each other easily—they've got a connection that has to go beyond this life."

WHEN THE BUSHWHACKERS MOVED ON from their camp in the field, it was Hester who came to retrieve Eben. He and Kip were sitting at the table quietly working on fixing an oil lamp; Kip held the lamp in place while Eben threaded the metal tools through the small burner, when the knock came at the backdoor.

Both men rose.

"Yes?" Kip asked, with the door still closed.

"It's me."

Kip opened the door and Hester stood before them. Eben watched Kip study her a moment, but she avoided his gaze. Then Hester looked around Kip at Eben.

"You can come home now," she said to him.

"Hester," her name came out as a whisper on Kip's lips. "How have you been?" Eben went to the side of the room to collect his pack and bedroll. There was a long silence that filled the room.

"Say something," Kip commanded. "Say something, Hester."

"Why should I?" Hester snapped. "Why should I say anything when all you have been is silent for years?"

Eben stopped readying himself for departure to listen.

"How could you just sit here all that time? How can you just stand here now?" Hester's voice was the disgusted tone of someone so hurt and so surprised by it.

"How can you suffer this? How could you not come to be with me when you returned from the war? You want me to say something when you said nothing to me all this time? No, I will not." Hester turned away from Kip, but then quickly turned back. "You left me alone. After all this is over, how will you think of yourself? Will you be a proud man? You are the biggest disappointment of my life." Hester turned again and walked away from the house.

"That did not go as I had imagined it might," Kip said, and walked back to the table.

Eben grabbed his pack and hurriedly stuffed his loose articles inside.

"Thank you for letting me stay here. If you would let me, I could come back and help finish with the projects we have discussed."

"There is no need," Kip said, and started to put away the unfixed lantern.

"I wouldn't mind. Thank you again."

Eben went to leave but turned one more time to Kip, as Hester had done. "I admit, if I were in your position, I would spend my life wondering what I missed more, my arm or her."

Kip moved his hand into the space where his arm had been, as if feeling for something only he could see.

MARLOW

A company of Yankee traitors tracked us. They get Decker as we start to leave the McClouds' house on the other side of the wide river. They open up on him. The impact of the bullets keeps him in a kind of dance for a moment on the slab of the front door, jerking about before he falls. It is fair game to kill a man this way, but indecent to spray him with such fire when he is long gone. Their vanity leaves them reloading while we fire our way out of the house and make for the horses tied to a group of trees south of the hog pen. We have seen more fights end poorly for those left inside a structure than for those on free ground running. No one thinks to try and take Decker's body. We have seen too much of that sentiment as well, and know when you need to scoot rather than lolly.

Royal crouches low through the weeds, having slid out of a side window, and makes it across to the field first, as the rest of us, clustering in small numbers behind even smaller obstructions, try to find a way to get the horses. Royal spectaculars by climbing a birch tree like some monkey phantom and from that location he picks off the Jayhawkers like sun searching for the forest floor. They don't know where the shots are coming from, and they fall like timber logs where they stand.

While Royal clears our path we make a run for it, some of our men fall, but many of us make it across the clearing. We are able to get close enough that we can reach out to our horses' reins, but we didn't expect the men to be waiting for us there, and as my hands touch the saddlebag I am damn near shot in the face by some Red Leg standing between mine and Boston's ride, but the Yank is the unfortunate one, for Boston rushes up beside us and hits him across the head with his pistol butt, and as he falls Boston fires one into the man's chest. Boston is the kind of man who stops to regard his direct kills. I spend a moment regarding it alongside him, and then we focus our attention on staying alive.

Although we are all using guns, it feels like we are in hand-to-hand combat. My blood beats a rhythm. We see who we shoot and how they collapse and then we step over their bodies in our advance. Smoke fills all the spaces where men aren't falling. Both sides are blended, spread out on the property, shooting whatever shoots at them until they are shot at no more. I am up on my horse and pullin' him out of this fight. There is ringing in my ears as the hammer of my gun hits the pallet.

Royal and I find our way to each other down the road and it doesn't need saying, we ride away from our comrades into the woods with no farewell words. This was as good a time as any to part ways.

WE CIRCLE BACK TO MY family's land and it is late in the day when we reach it. Hester meets us in the yard before we even have time to dismount.

"Aimee is gone," she says.

"What do you mean she's gone?" Royal asks.

"Yesterday she said she was going for a walk before it became too dark and she never came back."

"Did you look for her?" I question.

"Of course we did. Eben and the boys have been out there all morning."

Royal turns his horse and rides off toward one of the wood paths.

"You stay here until someone comes back," I tell my sister. "Don't go off by yourself."

"Marlow," she says my name but that is all.

"I know," I say. The trouble that has befallen Aimee could have so easily happened to my sister and she knows it. "We'll find her."

I turn my horse away from the sun and follow the path up the creek bed toward the fields where people go to collect flowers for their sweethearts.

CHAPTER

TWENTY

HESTER

It did not take long for Marlow to find Aimee below the branches of a large river oak farther down the creek. She hung from a noose. The rope tied to a high thick limb that creaked lightly at the weight of her body. There was blood smeared down the front of her skirt, for her wrists had also been cut.

"Why would they have done that?" Hester asked, when her brother led her to Aimee. "Why would they have killed her twice?" No one had any answers.

Marlow, Royal and Eben worked together to bring her down. They set her upright against the tree. Royal sat down beside Aimee. He put his legs out in front of him the way Aimee's were spread. He rested his head back and then tipped it to the side so it lightly touched hers. Royal looked down at her hands that had naturally cupped themselves one on top the other as if something was held there, but they were empty. Royal took the right hand in his and held it. The moment was too much for the others and they had to take a step and turn away. Hester was glad that she made the boys stay at the house. Although this was deep love, it was also haunting.

"She should have seen this," Marlow said.

"Perhaps she did see it," Eben offered. "Perhaps she saw the futures clear and this darkness was better than another."

"Oh, you shut up," Marlow spat.

But Eben finished, "Perhaps she gave up one fate for another."

Hester did not believe in the equation of loss, but in this moment she thought she could feel Royal's spirit detach from him and knew it would never again connect with his body. No matter where he'd go, his true self would always follow him like a shadow. This is what happened at the loss of your half, the one your heart was most joined with.

The men lifted Aimee's body on to the quilt they brought with them. Royal cupped her head gently in his hands. Marlow helped him carry her out of the woods. Hester led the horses. The boys had come from the house when they saw them cross the field. Knowing what was being brought to them, Steven ran around the house to sit away from them on the front porch. Aaron burst into tears and burrowed himself in the cloth of Hester's skirt, and after they set the body down on the porch and the blanket fell away and exposed Aimee's colorless face, Lonnie too started to whimper. Eben pulled the boy to him and tried to soothe him. Hester looked over to Royal, who stood next to the porch with his hand on Aimee's hand.

"Royal." She stopped after she said his name because she was suddenly unsure of the words to use for what needed to be said.

"Royal," Marlow spoke for her. "Bury or burn?"

After a moment Royal answered. "Burn," he decided. "The wind will bring her to the sea."

Everyone went to gather kindling for the pyre they would make for Aimee. They had no extra clothes to fancy themselves for the mourning or adorn the body for the service. Hester helped Royal remove Aimee's coverall dress, and her feminine form lay silently in her white thin slip. Hester brought Royal a cloth and a bowl of water and he bathed his beloved.

They piled the collected wood in the middle of field and Marlow pulled his sister aside.

"This is not going to be pleasant. We should not do this near our plot. The smell is going to be something I can't describe. The ash will fall upon us."

"Then let her rain down on us," she said to him. "Start seeing this loss like the rest of us, Marlow, or you will fall too far behind."

IT WAS DARK WHEN THEY gathered around Aimee's body on the pyre they made for her and set the wood ablaze. The flames reached up and curled around her

156

body. The fire sounded its cackle. As the flames lit up the faces of those around her, Hester saw Steven appear out of the dark—she could see the lines that had been created where his tears had washed the dirt from his cheeks. Hester shook away the thought that the image looked like warpaint and was thankful that the boy was with them even if just outside their group. That whole day Royal made hardly a sound.

HESTER READIED THE BOYS FOR sleep. She read to them from one of their storybooks but she could tell she did not have their attention. She continued for a while anyway until Aaron stopped her.

"What will happen to Aimee now that she is dead?"

Hester did not know but couldn't tell them that.

"She will go somewhere else," she told them. She knew that was not enough. Hester never saw the dead the way it was said some could. Her mother had never visited her after death, and Hester never felt her father's presence, though he must have been dead for some time now. That was not something she could offer the children. She closed the book on her lap and stood up.

"Will she visit us like Steven's brother visits him?" Aaron wondered.

"Maybe."

"If I talk to her, can she still hear me?" Lonnie asked.

"Yes, she will hear you," Eben said, coming into the room.

"This is your fault," Steven said to Eben from where he sat leaning against the wall near the sofa. "If you hadn't come back, she would still be alive."

"Steven, do not talk like that," Hester said.

"You tell us to tell the truth. I am saying it."

"You don't see all the parts of it," Hester told him.

"You always take his side," Steven said, balling up his fists by his sides and giving the wall a punch.

"I am not taking anyone's side."

"The soldiers should have stayed. They would have protected her," Steven said.

"They weren't soldiers and there wasn't anything they could have done," Hester told him. "They would have just been killed themselves. Our field would become a graveyard."

"You don't know that!" Steven yelled.

"Be quiet, Steven!" Hester yelled back. Hester never raised her voice in front of the boys and it startled them all. Hester composed herself. "We are all tired. I would like us to get some rest now. In the morning, we shall still be sad, but we will have more energy to grieve with." Hester tucked Lonnie and Aaron into their couch bed. She did not go near Steven, who stayed seated on the floor and pulled his knees up to his chest.

"What's grieve?" Aaron asked.

"Grief is the feeling of wanting something you can't have," Hester told him. "And no matter what, you'll never have it."

Hester stayed with the boys awhile longer. When she made her way up to her room, Steven still sat wide awake, glaring at her.

HESTER WOKE IN THEIR BED just as Steven was bringing a knife down on Eben's chest. Eben had heard the boy come into the room, but Hester had not. Eben grabbed the boy's wrist, stopping the motion just as the tip of the knife cut into the skin.

"Steven," Eben said firmly. Hester did not move. Her arm was over Eben's bare stomach, and she could see the blade just a foot from her face. She couldn't see Steven, but could hear his breath deep on the exhale. She watched Eben's face. She searched for fear, but he showed none.

"Brother says you were on the other side," Steven whispered. "That the war is over, but it has not been settled up. He says there is still harm to be had." He tightened his grip on the knife.

"Steven," Eben said his name again, softer this time. "I am on this side now. The side of this house. This side with Hester here. And this side with you. I will look after you. I will keep walking you to school and keep meeting you at the end of the day until you tell me you are too old and ask to go alone." He spoke faster now with his promises. "I will teach you to hunt with a trap and to hook crawfish. I will show you anything I know; dancing, which fork to use when, how to skip stones in a muddy creek." He paused. "Your brother doesn't need to look out for you anymore. If he'll let me, I'd like to do that for you. But we both can't do it. You ask him if he'll give the job over to me now. You tell him I'll do my very best."

Eben released his hold on Steven's wrist. Steven moved the knife up and out, revealing the slight puncture wound. Eben winced. Steven took a step back, then set the knife down on the side of the bed.

"I'm going to sleep now," Steven said. He left the room as silently as he slipped in. Hester reached up and touched the spot of blood on Eben's chest.

"I didn't know you could dance," she said.

HESTER HAD LONNIE AND AARON escort her when she went into town to make trades for flour and yeast. She sent them to Mrs. Walsh's with a few coins she got off Marlow to buy some wool, while she went into Mr. Jeremy's shop.

"I have heard some very unpleasant rumors," Mr. Jeremy said to Hester when she entered the store.

"In these times, they are probably not rumors."

160

"They killed Mr. Boston and most of his men just north of the William Parish Bridge."

"Let's just settle the trade."

"Many Union went down in the fight, two local Jay-hawkers among them."

"What can I get for these jams?" Hester said, pointing to the items she had displayed in front of him. The jams had been from a batch Aimee had made and it was not easy for her to part with them.

"And there is talk that—"

"Please, just give me what I came for and let me go," Hester begged.

"I'm sorry, Hester, usually we make talk," Mr. Jeremy said, as he hurried to examine the items she brought with her.

"I'm sorry," Hester said and covered her mouth. She tried to compose herself, though she knew tears were forming in the corners of her eyes. "I'm so sorry I reacted like that."

"Don't be sorry, I shouldn't have spoken loosely. She was your friend," Mr. Jeremy said.

"You already know?" Hester asked. "How could you already know?"

Mr. Jeremy slipped the bag of flour and a pouch of yeast into her basket and added a few strips of jerky in with them, because he always gave her more than she deserved.

"People talk," he told her. "It's what they've always done.

It's what they will always do. In this town, it is not far for the words to go before they fall upon another's ears."

"Of course, this town is all talk and no one is going to do anything about it."

"I did not know your friend, but she seemed like a pleasant lady."

"She was."

"You keep yourself safe, Hester."

Hester nodded and collected her basket.

She was not but a foot out the door when Kip approached her.

"Hester, may I speak to you?"

She felt her cheeks flush and this stomach turn over, but she was exhausted. She just stood there and waited for him to speak further.

"Hester, do you still want me?" Kip asked.

She smiled then at the thought that of all the days to have this conversation, he had decided on this one. Her pairing with him would have been wrong, even if there had been no war. A part of her would have felt it eventually, she would have realized she wanted a man who shared his caring differently than Kip would be able to. She did not feel angry with him anymore. Aimee's death had muted many of her emotions; she was now just tired and sad.

"I think that I am ready now," Kip said.

"You were not there for me," she said calmly.

"I was no good for you after this happened." He pulled the stub of his arm up.

"You could have let me decide that. I cannot stand beside someone who is only there for me when he feels like it. I need someone to try even if he's got nothing at all."

"That sounds a little selfish, Hester."

"Kip, I don't deserve less than that."

"But I am ready now. I needed time for myself after all I had been through. But I am ready now. You don't need anyone else."

She wanted to tell him that the feelings already settled in. That it didn't matter that another man had stirred her heart. The memory of Kip not coming to her when she was most desperate was how she saw him now. She wouldn't forgive him for that.

"You made me wait years for you." Hester felt as if she was being released from a bond that was held for long enough. "I'm sorry, there is nothing left for you now." And she would offer no more.

As she walked across the town toward where the boys were waiting for her, their basket filled with yarn where the eggs had been, she passed Cody Brinson's house. He sat on his porch chair; his feet rested up on the rail.

"Why hello, Hester," he called to her, this man who as a boy would not have glanced at her and before the war would not have risked disrespecting her. She stopped but did not turn to him. "Interesting turn of events. We came looking for you and found her instead," he said of Aimee. "Maybe we tried hangin' her and she just wouldn't depart. Maybe we found her half-dead and did her the extra lot. Perhaps you'll never know. Perhaps we'll never say. She was a beaut, that is certain. As are you, Hester Cain. As are you."

Hester felt the deep hickory in the throat, and the swaying willow in her chest. Out of the corner of her eye she saw Cody sitting with that crabgrass between his teeth, rocking the heels of the chair on the wood. It wasn't just revenge she wanted, but the absence of his presence. She didn't want his eyes on her, and she didn't want him walking around as if he had a right to all the corners of Missouri. She had enough of his take-without-asking ways. If him gone meant blood on the hem of her dress so be it. His death would do.

CHAPTER
TWENTY-ONE

MARLOW

When Hester comes into the kitchen, Royal and I are already cleaning our guns.

"Marlow."

"Yes, Hester?"

"It is time to take care of Cody," she tells me matter-of-fact, setting down her basket. "This needs ending. Either way."

"Consider it done," I say.

My sister has just told me to kill a man and I am proud of her for it.

"I'll be going with you." Eben emerges from the front room. Royal and I exchange a coded look between us, caught and broken. Bush fighting was not like no other warrin', we only watch the backs of our own, and sometimes not even that. There is no room for spectators.

"I can't be having that man coming into this house whenever he pleases," Eben says.

"You all go and you handle this," Hester charges. "You come back before dawn."

WHEN DARKNESS FALLS, EBEN, ROYAL and I take the horses the long way around into town. Eben rides one of the horses that had followed me home from when I killed the Union men at the old Bushwhacker hideout. The horse has a lazy walk and he keeps having to encourage it along to keep up with us.

"How many will be in the house?" Eben asks.

"Can't say," I tell him. Usually, it is just Royal and me, we walk our horses gentle-like, and we don't need to talk. We don't need a plan.

"We aren't just going to break the door down," Eben attempts to confirm.

"Yes. We are," I say.

"We will watch the house, then we'll go in," Eben strategizes.

"Suddenly think someone made you leader?" I say. Royal keeps out of it.

"I like the thought of waiting until it's three on one, than three on an unknown number that could cut us down," Eben says. "I want to be able to go home to Hester, don't you?"

"We got to make a stop and then we'll talk some more about you calling all the rules now," I say curtly.

We tie our horses up to Mr. Jeremy's fence. I see him open his curtains, then close them again. We walk behind the houses, around the pens and fences, until we reach Kip's cabin. I knock three times paced and slow. He opens the door. I let myself in.

"Hello, Marlow," he says.

"We've come to settle things with Cody Brinson, care to join us?" I ask.

"You removing him won't end it," Kip tells me.

Royal follows me in and silently goes to stand by the back window to peer out the crack in the shutters.

"It ends some of it," I say.

"They'll come for you."

"Better than Cody coming for us first," Eben says, as he emerges through the door.

"You're going as well?" Kip asks. Eben nods.

"A group of them rode out of here this afternoon, heard there were some returning Confederate soldiers being marched through Jefferson," Kip informed us. "Cody didn't go with them. The men won't return until the day after to-morrow. Now's as good a night as any, I suppose."

"Still, we should watch the house for awhile and make sure he's alone," Eben leads.

I have Eben by the throat before he sees me coming. I push him down so his back is flat on the eating table. I hold one of his arms over his head. Eben punches at my stomach with his free hand, and kicks wildly at me with his legs, but I got him in a tight lock.

"Stop trying to be the boss-man," I spit in his face. "Stop trying to tell us how it's all going to be." My grip on his neck is so tight his face, which was red when I first grabbed him, is now paling.

Royal stands back and watches, but Kip steps in and inserts his shoulder between us and tries to shove us apart.

"Look what he's about to do," Kip pleads with me. "He's not one of us, but he's not one of them. He has settled here and has become a Missouri man. Enough to kill to keep his way of life as he wishes it."

Eben's punches are coming with less strength now. He is dying and I am willing it to be so.

"Marlow," Royal says my name faintly, but I hear him and look up. "Your choice has already been made for you by Hester," Royal says. "You cannot change it now."

I think of all that I must not let down. I must be true to the Cause, to my comrades, to my lost Pa, but most of all who I must not fail is Hester, to her I must be loyal above all else. I picture Hester in my mind and what her face would look like if Eben did not return with us. And that is all it takes for me to ease my grip on Eben's throat. He pushes me away, grasps at his neck as he stands a few feet from me, trying to catch his breath.

I go to the window and pull the curtain aside. I watch the town. It is quiet. Only a little movement inside the houses across the road. There is a light shining from a downstairs window of Cody Brinson's house. I turn back to those in the room. I watch Kip bring Eben a cup of water to drink.

"Well, aren't you two just the pals now," I hiss.

We watch Cody's house for an hour. One shadow moves around inside it with a singular light. Then we watch the glow move across the room, up the stairs to the second floor. After the time it would take for a man to undress, get into his warm bed, and pull the quilt up tight to his chin, the light goes out.

"Maybe I'll get lucky and Cody will shoot you," I say, turning to Eben.

"Hester will still blame you for my death," Eben tells me. He talks as if we are discussing any ol' thing. "She may not say it, but a part of her will resent you, that part of her that would wonder if it was you who pulled the trigger. That long-standing sibling bond will get you back in the house, yes, but my death would eat at her and create her doubt in you."

"We've known that girl always," I remind him. "Don't talk to us like we don't know how she'd perceive every this-that-which-way outcome. What could you know about her that we do not?" I ask.

Eben stands very still.

"What I'm sure of Hester is this: she is afraid of everything. And this: she is afraid of everything, but she doesn't let it stop her for nothing," he tells us. "She is afraid of big spiders and bats and prayers not working and prayers working, and the dark, and death and starving, and being alone, and deep winter. She is afraid of Grant and Lee, and of being a mother. She is afraid of so much, but what Hester is not afraid of is love and loving, and that is something so powerful that it illuminates all those other fears and makes seeing through them possible because she has this strength on her side. If she wills it enough, it shadows her doubts and hopelessness and nerves. It is a mighty silencer." Then Eben turns toward Kip. "And I'm sure she'd have loved you with no limbs."

THERE IS ONLY ONE MAN in the house. Eben and Royal are hidden in a cluster of trees behind the Brinson place. Kip and I are in the shadows under the awning of the icehouse across the street.

"If this goes not in my favor, you got to look after Hester," I tell Kip.

"I don't think she'll have me now," he says.

"No, she will not. But you look after her just the same."

With a bird call we commence on the house at the same time, Eben and Royal through the back door, Kip and I through the front.

As Kip and I knock in the front door with our boot heels, we are not two feet in the door when Cody starts sending shots down to us from the upstairs. The house is dark except for the light our gunfire makes. The smoke from our guns lifts up the stairs reaching for the ceiling of the house, but it's trapped from escape.

After a minute there is a pause in the firing.

"Is that you, Marlow?" I hear Cody call down.

"You know it is," I shout up.

Kip keeps guard of the main street, Eben the back yard. Royal and I come together in the middle of the house and apply cover fire for each other as we ascend the stairs. The shooting is sporadic. A few townspeople will open their doors to investigate the noise and Kip will gesture for them to go back inside. No one is coming to anyone's aid.

Cody tries to escape from us through the window, but when he jumps from the second floor, Eben is waiting for him. Cody slowly rises from the crouched position he has landed in.

"Why are you here? Why are you with them?" Cody questions Eben's allegiance, surprised to find the man with me.

Eben raises his gun. I come and stand out on the roof. Maybe Cody is begging, but I can't hear anything that he says.

"You going to kill him, Eben?" I call down.

"I am thinking I might," he says. But he doesn't act on impulse. I hear Royal come through the back door and stand directly below me.

"Well, go on then," I say.

And with that Eben shoots Cody Brinson in the head, a direct kill. He returns his pistol to his holster.

No one says anything. Kip walks back to his home, and Eben, Royal and I walk down the other road to where our horses are tied.

CHAPTER
TWENTY-TWO

HESTER

Hester watched the rebuild take place on the plot all morning. She wondered if the work on the new barn would distract their other thoughts and give calm to their days. Hester walked over to where Steven was attempting to tug free a beam from a stack of used wood.

"Steven, your brother around?" Hester asked.

"No. He's not around," Steven told her. "He's gone."

"Gone where?"

"I don't know," Steven said, and let go of his tugging match. "Where people go when they're gone."

Hester rubbed her forehead.

"You think he's coming back?"

"Can't say." Steven shrugged.

"If he does, you point him out."

"Alright."

"Alright?" she questions him again.

"Yes, alright."

The boy's advancement to clear the darkness had been slow since he stabbed Eben, but there had been progress.

Hester went onto the porch. Eben sat on a chair, taking a rest from the sun's heat, a thick piece of tree trunk before him acting as a table for the wood board he had upon it. He whittled his knife against the lumber. He moved over a smidge indicating that she could sit down and share the chair with him. She did so.

"Thank you," Hester said.

"What needs thanking?" Eben asked, as he kept at the wood with the knife, digging in.

"Going to town with Marlow and Royal. What you did there. And for stopping here in the first place. It couldn't have been an easy choice."

"You make it an easy choice."

"I know it may not be over," Hester told him. "That things won't just suddenly be safe and simple, but I feel you will still want to stay on, even with my brother here."

"Of course I'll be staying, Hester, if that's good with you. If that is good with Marlow."

"He and I discussed it and came to an agreement that he wouldn't kill you."

"What was said exactly?"

"I said, 'Marlow, you can't kill him ever,' and my brother said, 'I promise I won't kill him.'"

"And that's good enough for you?"

"That is good enough for me."

"Shall I stay then?"

Eben spent these seasons teaching her about the land so she'd never be without again, and she beheld him and their home now with such possibility.

"What skills do you have to offer us?" Hester asked Eben.

"Skills?"

"What had you learned before you learned warrin'?" It was a strange thing to ask after all their time together, but she wanted reassurance like the speech he offered Steven when the boy tried to kill him. Eben indulged her.

"I know chickens, I know fox, I know garden, small plow. I know fire and roof."

"That's good," Hester said, giving him a nod of satisfaction from his answer. She looked back out at the field where Marlow was reshaping wood from the destroyed shed to make the beginnings of the frame for the new structure.

"You want to know what I know since warrin'?" Eben asked her.

"What do you know since warrin'?"

"I know you," he said.

They gave each other a small smile. Hester nudged him with her elbow. Hester's heart beat hard and steady.

"What's that you're making?" she asked.

"A small wood chest," Eben told her. "A place for you to put your hope in."

Eben stood up and went into the yard where Steven was dragging the large piece of timber toward Marlow. Eben picked up the end that dragged on the ground and together they carried it the remainder of the way.

Royal appeared from the house. He put his long arms up and touched a beam from the roof. He supported his weight and leaned forward a little off the edge of the porch. Hester watched Aaron and Lonnie in the field as they walked the horses down toward the creek.

"I haven't a good hold on him no more," Hester said to Royal of her brother.

"You got hold enough," Royal told her.

"You and I could steady him."

"His impulse to kill can be triggered by a sleight of hand and is something to watch out for," Royal said. "It could be dormant a long time, then a whisper could set him off."

Marlow's desire to go out hunting was strong. It could always be there, that want. It could be kept quiet, Hester was sure of it, with her stepping into the kitchen before he decided whom to kill. With her asking him to bring in wood for the fire before he could pick his weapon. With her smiling at him before he could load his gun. Royal could sense it. He read her brother's thoughts, as she could. "Get out of your head," he'd be able to say to Marlow if he were here, though he too would be holding in an impulse. Revenge could rise in them both and Hester knew it.

"No one's going to hang themselves from that structure," Royal promised Hester. He spoke as if he inherited Aimee's sight. The memory of the loss hit Hester's chest heavy but for a moment, then it settled in, and she felt it pass.

Royal asked, "Do you want me to take the boy Steven with me when I go?"

"No. I think he should stay," Hester told him. "As should you."

"This isn't a place I know how to be from," Royal said, weary of being swallowed by missing his love. They both observed the land. Hester didn't feel it was damaged, nor was it a gift.

"And still," she said. "You will belong."

"And still," Royal mirrored her words.

Hester didn't continue the conversation. Instead, she sat in the silence, and witnessed the slow build of their new life begin to take shape.

ABOUT THE AUTHOR

LIBBY COPA is an author, educator, and future nomad. Her work has appeared in publications across the country, including *Hanging Loose, Sin Fronteras, DASH, Matter, Hobart, Quail Bell Magazine, The Blue Mountain Review,* and *Monday Night Lit.*

You can connect with Libby online at:

W W W . L I B B Y C O P A . C O M

@LibbyCopa

Also by Libby Copa

Rebel Writer's Workbook
Your Creative Path Workbook

DESERT ANIMAL

Made in the USA
Monee, IL
18 July 2023

39475927R00111